Which Bird Are You?

Which Bird Are You?

Merrick Rosenberg

WhichBirdAreYou.com
MerrickRosenberg.com
TakeFlightLearning.com

MerrickRosenberg.com
WhichBirdAreYou.com
ChiefParrot@TakeFlightLearning.com

ISBN: 978-0-9964110-6-6
e-ISBN: 978-0-9964110-7-3

Cover art and interior layout by Copper Owl Press (Kaytalin McCarry)

Published in the United States of America

For my parents,
my wife, Traci,
and my children, Gavin and Ben,
you taught me what it means
to be a good human being.

CHAPTER ONE

The 5th grade class at Galen Elementary had waited years for this moment. Today, it was finally their turn. In the spring of their final year at the school, students would spend a week at Camp Discovery. Sure, there were nature classes and science experiments to tackle, but they had been looking forward to this since first grade. No parents. No homework. No chores! Just fun with their friends in the woods.

Following a two-hour drive to camp, the students filed off the bus. Serena, with her wavy black hair and gentle smile, was first off the bus. She spent the past week worried about what would happen at Camp Discovery. Which girls would be in her cabin? Would she have to compete in sports games? She much preferred spending time quietly with her close friends.

Caleb followed just behind her. His tall, thin frame was capped with clean-cut, light brown hair and a logical, curious mind. What kind of science experiments will they do? He loved science. Will they have telescopes? While viewing the dark night sky, far away from city lights, maybe Caleb would see the Milky Way he'd read about in astronomy books. Will they study the earth? Maybe Caleb could add to his already sizable collection of gems, minerals, and fossils. He was ready for an exciting week.

Serena and Caleb enjoyed chatting on their way to the camp. And Ms. Allport, their science and math teacher, enjoyed listening to their thoughtful conversation. This was Ms. Allport's fourteenth trip to Camp Discovery, and she was well-prepared. In fact, she packed a week ago to ensure she wouldn't forget anything. Her clear plastic containers of science equipment were neatly labeled and stacked in alphabetical order in the cargo hold beneath the bus. She couldn't help but worry about them. What if the beakers broke? Did she pack them with enough foam padding? She wanted to make this week an experience that her students would remember fondly throughout their lives.

For many of the students, this would be the first time they spent a night in nature. Some felt anxious about leaving their phones behind at home. Serena and Caleb reached into their pockets out of habit, expecting the familiar touch of a phone case. As the fifth graders filed off the bus, they looked up at the tall trees, inhaled the pine air, and heard birds calling and responding, as if led by an orchestra conductor.

Iona was the second to last student to exit. Her long,

brown hair seemed to sport a new streak of color every month—this time the dye kit said, "Wild Orchid." Iona brought her aloha spirit with her everywhere. Her t-shirt read, "I didn't do it!" Bursting with energy, she leapt off the bus in typical Iona fashion and declared, "I made it. Let the games begin!"

Dominic, or just "Dom" to his friends, wasn't about to be outdone by Iona. He reached the last step and paused for a moment to survey the campground. "Let's do this!" Dom said, as if he could give permission for the festivities to begin. With short brown hair to match his short brown body, Dom wore his confidence like a superhero costume with muscles built into the fabric. He liked to be in charge and, whenever possible, he usually was.

A crew of eight teaching assistants busily unloaded the week's supplies from the cargo hold and onto golf carts. Mr. Marston, the social studies and language arts teacher, called the students to attention. Tall and loud, Mr. Marston could seem larger than life, especially next to the soft-spoken Ms. Allport. Although he almost always sported a smile, each had a different meaning. He could express confidence, joy, or concern with the smallest of movements. Mr. Marston and Ms. Allport were a great team, and the kids loved both of them.

Mr. Marston sorted everyone into two groups of boys and

two groups of girls. Each would have their own cabin staffed by two teaching assistants. They carried their sleeping bags and gear to their homes for the week.

The four green-roofed cabins seemed camouflaged in the forest. Each one had its own distinct garden.

Dom, of course, marched out front and reached his cabin first. In front of the covered porch, a log fence surrounded four boulders sitting in sand. Two wooden statues stood proudly in the center: One of a young girl with her hands on her hips, and one of a young boy pointing towards the sky as if directing people to look upwards. As Dom stepped through the door, he said, "Welcome to my castle."

As Caleb approached his cabin, he noticed rows and columns of plants lined up with laser precision. In the center, a metal sundial measured the passage of time. The scene created a feeling of order and structure. Caleb knew that someone must have spent countless hours to create something like this. That impressed him.

As Iona approached her cabin, she was delighted to see a garden filled with playful wildflowers. The bright yellows, reds, and oranges made it look like the ground was on fire. The seeming randomness of the arrangement added rather than subtracted from the beauty, in Iona's opinion.

Before entering her cabin, Serena paused to admire a tranquil fountain beside a cobblestone path. The stones flowed towards an oak bench where she could sit quietly to read or talk with a friend. The copper fountain burbled consistently, giving the same amount of water and the same steady chorus of splashes with each moment.

After the students unloaded their belongings, they gathered for orientation at the mess hall, where they went over the rules of Camp Discovery. The students learned that, above all else, they must respect themselves, each other, and the property. Serena and Caleb listened intently. Dom crossed his arms and wondered why this was necessary. Iona, meanwhile, played soccer with sugar packets.

They also reviewed the week's agenda. They'd spend each day learning, participating in sports, and engaging in nature hikes and activities at the lake. At night, they would gather at a campfire in the amphitheater.

After orientation, the group lined up at the food counter for hamburgers, hotdogs, French fries, and bug juice. Nobody knew why it was called "bug juice," and nobody wanted to ask.

Following lunch, the group walked to a grassy area near the tennis courts. Iona spied a groundskeeper putting the finishing touches on a row of shrubs. With the sunlight bouncing off his silver hair, he trimmed the hedge to form a perfect rectangle around the courts. Iona called to the groundskeeper, "Cool shrubs!" He smiled politely and continued his work.

When they arrived at their destination, Ms. Allport instructed the students to form a circle and waited patiently for them to comply. She looked like a referee with a whistle around her neck, a clipboard in one hand, and two Hula Hoops in the other.

Standing at the center of the circle, Ms. Allport asked everyone to take the hands of the people next to them. She approached two of the students and instructed them to release each other's hands. She placed one of the hoops between them and instructed the two students to reach their hands through the center of the hoop to reconnect.

Ms. Allport walked directly across the circle and placed another Hula Hoop between two other students. She returned to the center and addressed the pair who held the first Hula Hoop. "Here's the plan," she said. "You must move that Hula Hoop around the circle without disconnecting your hands. You'll have to step through the hoop. The goal is to make your Hula Hoop catch up with the other one."

All the of the children replied, "Noooo!"

She turned to the other pair. "That Hula Hoop is going to try to catch yours. Are you going to let it?"

Ms. Allport then addressed the entire group. "Are you ready?"

The students all nodded as Iona shouted an exuberant, "Yes!"

"On three," Ms. Allport said. "One. Two. Three. Go!"

The students quickly weaved through the hoops, some head first, some feet first. Some hoops momentarily caught on shoulders, heads, knees, and ankles, but the hoops kept chasing each other. They seemed closer and farther at times, but they never met.

After a few minutes of cheering and laughter, Ms. Allport blew the whistle, and the activity came to a halt. Before Ms. Allport could ask a question, Dom called out, "So who won?"

"What a great question. I will answer your question with some questions of my own. And I'd like you all to shout out your answers as loud as you can. First, how many students are here?"

Dom did a quick count and yelled out, "Thirty-two!"

"That's right. And how many cabins do we have?"

All of the students shouted, "Four!"

"Excellent," Ms. Allport replied. "And how many Hula Hoops are there?"

"Two!"

"Here's my last question. How many groups are here at the camp?" Some students looked puzzled. Caleb glanced side to side before he questioningly answered, "One?"

"Correct," the teacher said. "All together. How many groups are here?"

"One!!!" the students shouted even louder.

"That's right. We are one group. Not four. Not two. One. We are here to share this experience together. We are here to support each other and learn as one connected group."

Dom called out to Ms. Allport, "But who won?"

"Well, can anyone tell me the goal of this activity?"

"To win?" Dom called out.

"To have fun? Iona added.

Ms. Allport nodded in agreement. "What else?"

Caleb raised his hand and answered, "To move the Hula Hoop around the circle by stepping through it without disconnecting our hands. Our goal was to make that one Hula Hoop catch the other."

"Keep going," said Ms. Allport. "We're almost there."

Serena raised her hand so that only her fingertips poked above her head. When called upon, she suggested, "Work together?"

"Yes!" Ms. Allport exclaimed.

"I see," said Caleb. "Instead of trying to keep the Hula Hoops away from each other, we could have moved them towards each other."

"Precisely. You win by working together. You have fun when you support one another. You achieve your goals when you act as one group. During this week, you will face many challenges. And I can tell you this: Working together will allow you to learn and grow—and yes, Dom, win together. So let's help each other and enjoy our time at Camp Discovery."

They spent the next part of the day doing various science experiments. First, they made bug spray, which provided welcome relief from the thirsty mosquitoes. They then made a sundial clock of Popsicle sticks. Everyone agreed it was a lot more fun than being back at Galen Elementary. Could the whole week be this carefree and easy?

CHAPTER TWO

Little did the students know how handy their homemade bug spray would be. They put it to use during their second activity, canoeing on the lake. Afterwards, they enjoyed a dinner of chicken nuggets, tater tots, and chocolate cake.

As sunset neared, the sky fizzed orange and purple. With headlamps and flashlights ready to go, the students followed the camp's well-worn trails to the amphitheater for their evening activity. At the bottom of a hill, rows of wooden benches surrounded a fire pit, which illuminated the grey stone walls of the amphitheater.

The fire logs were arranged in a lattice resembling the "#" key on their smartphones. The groundskeeper, admiring his creation, left the students to enjoy the warmth and glow.

The students took a few minutes to gaze into the flames and warm their hands. When Mr. Marston took his seat on a stool near the fire, everyone somehow knew to quiet down. Well, mostly everyone. It took a moment for Iona to notice that she was the only one still speaking.

"Tonight," Mr. Marston began, "I'm going to share the first part of a story my grandfather told me when I was your age. It's a story that might be more about you than the characters who lived it."

A loud pop behind him sent sparks in the air, and the crowd let out a simultaneous, "Oooh." He continued, "I remember sitting at a campfire just like this one with my parents and grandparents. My Grandpa Bill, a great and wise man, gave the gift of this story to me. He called it The Bird Tale, and now I give it to you."

Many moons ago, birds ruled the four corners of the continent Aviara. Eagles flew high above the fierce mountains in the northwest. Colorful parrots filled the air with chatter in the jungle trees of the northeast. A community of doves lived together in the southeast near wetlands. And owls watched for the smallest of movements in the low-lying woodlands of the southwest.

Gradually, human beings came to occupy Aviara. They had great respect for the birds who had come before them and honored their spirit through their cultures. The people learned from watching their flying friends. They observed their habits and attuned to their energy. In an effort to become one with the land and its creatures, they took on the characteristics of the birds.

In the northwest, people watched the eagles soar high above their nests on rocky cliffs. Each bird claimed a large territory and defended it. The people chose to do likewise, having observed the birds' strength. The Eagle Kingdom became a land of immense power. The people were independent and, like the birds who would dive at tremendous speeds to catch prey, they were willing to take big risks to get what they wanted. They displayed great confidence, and no other nation would dare challenge the Eagle Kingdom.

In the northeast, the Parrot Kingdom was filled with bustling activity. The birds were noisy, so people had to talk loudly to be heard. This land grew to be a boisterous place where people spent their days sharing stories and cracking jokes. Admiring the parrots' radiant feathers, the people dressed colorfully to match them. The birds gathered in large groups, so the people did the same. They enjoyed the excitement of their flying friends and created many festivals to celebrate even the smallest of occasions. Laughter, cheer, and music filled the air.

To the south of the Parrots, the Dove Kingdom was filled with peaceful streams and reflective lakes. The doves could often be seen gathering near the water. The people observed how the birds supported each other. If a predator came to attack, one of the doves would pretend to be injured to draw the predator away from the others. The birds nested close to each other, and the people did as well. The Dove Kingdom became a land of peace and harmony.

In the southwest, the Owl Kingdom was like no other. The Owls could pilot their dense forest at high speed, having noted the unique angle and position of every branch. Everything about the owl was sharp and accurate. From their talons to their keen eyesight, owls were creatures of precision. The people in this land made the owl ways their own. They became skilled architects, builders, and scientists. They were known to be deep thinkers and could be counted on for the quality of their work.

In addition to the four bird kingdoms, at the center of the continent was a small community of people who descended from the original settlers. Their land, known as Chamelia, was known for its local chameleons who could adapt to the environment around them. If a chameleon were sitting on a leaf, it would turn green. If it sat on a branch, it would turn brown.

The people of Chamelia modeled their world off the adaptable chameleon. Having gained familiarity with the people known as Eagles, Parrots, Doves, and Owls, they displayed the traits of each, as needed. Though few in number, the Chameleon people were revered by all. They embodied the Eagle's courage, the Parrot's joy of life, the Dove's compassion, and the Owl's logic. They adapted to every person and situation with ease.

Each of the four kingdoms had contact with Chamelia, but otherwise, they lived rather separately. Over time, the differences between the Eagles, Parrots, Doves, and Owls grew so wide they lost the ability to cooperate and communicate effectively with each other. This problem was overlooked until the time when four crises struck Aviara simultaneously. Unable to solve their shared problems, the four bird kingdoms placed their hopes with the Chameleons.

And so a representative, referred to as an

emissary, from each kingdom was dispatched from the four corners of the continent to discuss how they could work together. Eagleye came from the northwest. Nightowl came from the southwest. Dovetail journeyed from the southeast, and Parrotfeather wandered from the northeast. Like our own ancestors, the emissaries traveled by foot. Trains, cars, airplanes, and even horses did not yet exist in Aviara.

On a spring morning, the four emissaries met on common ground at the ancestral meeting place known as the Nest. This neutral land, which formed a ring around Chamelia, was not part of any kingdom. Whenever representatives from the bird kingdoms needed to speak with each other, they would meet here.

When a conversation was to be held with someone from Chamelia, per tradition, the Chameleon Ambassador would leave directions guiding the Eagle, Parrot, Dove, or Owl to a secondary location. They assumed this is where they would meet the Ambassador.

The emissaries arrived at the ancestral meeting place and found four towering wooden poles each bearing the flag of one of the kingdoms: red for

Eagles, yellow for Parrots, green for Doves, blue for the Owls, and purple for Chameleons. Nailed to the Chameleon flagpole was a map marking where they would retrieve further directions. From there, the group would journey together for two days into the heart of the continent where the Chameleon Ambassador awaited.

Things did not begin well. Nightowl arrived early and began studying the map. She was immediately followed by Dovetail. Eagleye arrived on time and was ready to leave as soon as she got there. "Let me see this," she said, snatching the map from Nightowl.

Unfortunately, Parrotfeather arrived a few minutes late because he took the "scenic route," not wanting to miss out on the marvels of Aviara.

Their differences became apparent immediately. Nightowl insisted they calculate the scale of the map by counting every step to the meeting ground and then converting it to miles. "Each of my steps is 2.2 feet long," said the Owl. "I assume you know your average stride lengths?"

Eagleye and Parrotfeather looked at Nightowl in disbelief. "Doesn't everybody?!" said Eagleye, not bothering to contain her sarcasm.

"Well, yes, every Owl would know that," insisted Nightowl.

Dovetail, upset by everyone's frustration, tried to make peace. "Perhaps we can start moving and count steps too?" he asked, not necessarily willing to tell others what they should do.

"Seriously," said Eagleye. "This is not complicated."

"Actually, it is quite complex," Nightowl insisted. "If you will draw your attention to the intersection labeled A, then you will clearly see…"

"…See that we're wasting time and ruining the adventure!" said Parrotfeather.

"Enough," said Eagleye. "We go now." She marched ahead with the map in hand, not bothering to check whether the group had followed.

Dovetail, already upset, walked quietly, eyes looking down at the brown, sandy soil. Parrotfeather regaled the other ambassadors with long stories about each and every sight he saw while they were waiting for him to arrive. Eagleye occasionally muttered "Uh-huh," not actually registering anything Parrotfeather said.

Nightowl couldn't take the stories anymore

and decided to walk at Dovetail's pace. She much preferred Dovetail's volume. Around midday, they reached their first destination. There stood four wooden statues.

Mr. Marston shook his head. "Wow. Sounds like they've got a lot of work ahead of them if they are going to bring Aviara together and save their people. Hold that memory of the statues until tomorrow night. It will be important. For now, let's see what happens when they meet the Chameleon Ambassador."

Two days after encountering the statues, the exhausted emissaries reached their destination in Chamelia. They spotted the Chameleon Ambassador in a grassy clearing wearing the traditional purple robes of her people. Green fields with colorful flowers stretched in all directions towards the horizon, leaving the travelers with a sense of possibility and freedom from their daily routines and assumptions.

The Ambassador was perched on an ornate chair made of ash, a wood known for its strength and flexibility. Rising up behind her, carved into the back of her chair, were an Eagle, Parrot, Dove, and Owl. A chameleon sat on each of their shoulders. The ambassador greeted the delegation. "Welcome to Chamelia. How were your travels?"

They all looked at each other, reluctant to share what it was really like to make the journey together. Dovetail forced a smile and said, "It was a long road, but we made it."

"Excellent," the ambassador exclaimed. "Just wonderful. Before we begin, take a moment to rest and recharge. Help yourself to some refreshments."

The Ambassador gestured towards a table set with five chairs and foods from all four of the bird kingdoms. There were also some delicacies unique to Chamelia and unknown to the weary travelers. The emissaries were glad to relax and regain their strength.

Once everyone was seated, the Ambassador began. "I want to get to know each of you. Tell me, which kingdom do you represent?"

Eagleye spoke first, proudly proclaiming that she hailed from the Eagle Kingdom. Eagleye looked at Dovetail, and with her eyes and a nod, told him to go next.

Dovetail said, "I am from the Dove Kingdom, and it is a profound honor to meet you."

Parrotfeather jumped in next, "I'm from the Parrot Kingdom, and I couldn't be happier to meet you!"

Nightowl closed out the introductions. "I am Nightowl, and as you have surely deduced, I am from the Owl Kingdom."

Mr. Marston took a deep breath and paused. Every student looked at him intently, eager for whatever would come next. "While I have been sharing the first part of The Bird Tale, Ms. Allport has been busy placing signs behind you. Each sign has an image of one of the birds. There is the sign for the confident and take-charge Eagle. Over here, you will find the sign for the talkative and social Parrots. In this direction, are the caring and sensitive Doves, and there are the accurate and logical Owls."

Mr. Marston continued, "If you could have lived on the continent of Aviara during the time of the four bird kingdoms, where would you have made your home? Would you have chosen to live with the Eagles, Parrots, Doves, or Owls? Stand up and head to the bird you identify with most."

The students made their way to the signs. Some of them knew exactly where to go. Others seemed to hesitate.

After a few moments, Mr. Marston's booming voice filled the amphitheater.

"Time out. Everyone freeze right where you are. For those of you who are having a difficult time picking one of the birds, let me tell you this. You all have a little bit of each bird's style within you. And there are times when you can be any one of them. You may feel like the Parrot as you cheer on your favorite sports team. There could be times when you are like the Dove as you listen to a friend who is upset. You could be an Owl when you do your homework or take a test at school. And you can be the Eagle when there is a problem and someone needs to take charge. But there is probably one bird that is most like you. That's the sign I want you to go to."

Dom had no trouble choosing the Eagle sign. "Eagles, get over here," he announced.

Iona called out to her fellow Parrots, "Come on, Parrots. Make some noise!"

The Doves, supported by Serena, and the Owls, including Caleb, waited patiently for instructions.

Once everyone had selected their kingdom, Mr. Marston asked the students to share a few examples of why they chose that particular bird and what that bird's style looks like in action. He gave the groups a few minutes to talk and then got their attention. "Okay everyone, which group would like to go first?"

Iona could barely contain her excitement. Her hand, along with every other Parrots', shot into the firelit air.

Mr. Marston knowingly grinned and said, "Parrots it is! Give us some examples of Parrots in action."

Iona began, "Well, if you haven't noticed, we like to be the center of attention."

Laughter echoed off the amphitheater walls. "We tell awesome stories, and we all agreed that we are better at talking than listening. Sometimes, we rush through chores because we want to get to things we enjoy. We're also great at cheering people on!"

Iona turned to her group and in unison, they said, "Gooooooo, Parrots!"

"I think they got it!" said Mr. Marston. "Who's next?"

Not to be outdone by the Parrots, Dom chimed in, "We'll go next."

"Okay Eagles, what do you have?"

"First off, we like a challenge and we like to win. We don't get distracted when we are working towards a goal. We make quick decisions and don't always like to follow rules. But hey, who follows all the rules anyway?"

Caleb whispered to a fellow Owl, "I do."

"Me too," his Owl friend replied.

"And we don't like being wrong," Dom added, "but then again, we're usually right, so that's not a big deal."

Iona, struggling to contain her chuckles, quietly commented, "Often wrong, but never in doubt."

Caleb raised his hand to go next. "We decided that we like to do things right—the first time. We like to plan things out before we do them and think through options that seem risky or dangerous."

Iona said a little too loudly, "Boooooooring."

Mr. Marston gave her a look that said, "Please don't interrupt."

Caleb continued, "And we like to think about things before we say them."

Iona wanted to comment on that too but resisted the temptation to speak, which, by the way, took a lot of effort.

"Finally," Caleb concluded, "we ask a lot of questions with our favorite being, 'Why?' We like to understand the world and questions help us do that."

"Perfect," Mr. Marston replied. "Very thorough, Owls."

He turned to the Dove team waiting patiently and asked them to share. Serena said, "We decided together that I will speak on the group's behalf. So here goes." She took a deep breath. "As the Doves, we like when people get along. Arguing makes us very uncomfortable. We try to be helpful whenever we can and we are very careful not to hurt people's feelings. We just think that everyone should be nice to each other. And we're really good listeners. Maybe that's because we're patient and we care about others."

Mr. Marston smiled. "You beautifully captured the Doves.

Thank you so much, Serena." He added, "Before we enjoy an incredible batch of hot apple cider, I have one last question: Which bird is the best?"

Without hesitation, the Parrot group chanted, "Paaaaarrots! Paaaaarrots! Paaaaarrots!"

With one commanding shout, the Eagles cheered, "EAGLES!"

The Owls thought about it for a moment. Caleb turned to his group to coordinate their answer. On a count of three, everyone in the Owl group simultaneously said, "Owls," in a voice that was neither loud nor soft.

The Doves didn't want to make anyone feel bad and remained silent.

Mr. Marston said, "I'll ask that question again later in the week, and we'll see if your answers change. For now, let's have some of the cider brewed by our amazing teaching assistants. We'll continue our story tomorrow."

Everyone headed over to a large pot sitting atop burning embers. The sweet smell of apples and spices filled the air. The group gazed into the fire as Caleb set his eyes to the Milky Way. It was truly a night to remember.

CHAPTER THREE

On Tuesday, the students awoke to sunlight filling their cabins. After a fun first day at Camp Discovery, they were excited for what the new day would bring. Following breakfast, the morning lesson began in the mess hall.

Ms. Allport got the students' attention by raising her right hand high into the air. It took a moment for the conversations to dwindle. Once everyone was listening, she announced that the group would spend its afternoon at the Camp Discovery Nature Center.

Iona was excited to play with the goats. She turned to Serena and said, "I heard about this thing called goat yoga. If they have goats that do yoga, I'm totally going to freak out."

Ms. Allport began, "In this morning's lesson, you will learn the art of orienteering. You will be given a map of your target destination where you will find a red flag. Think of the map as a bird's-eye view with north at the top. Imagine an eagle flying high above the land and looking down. This map is what the eagle sees."

The students were divided into eight groups of four, and each group was issued a compass. Ms. Allport explained the various parts of the compass: the baseplate in which the compass sits; the dial that surrounds the round device; the travel arrow that points in the desired direction; and finally, the magnetic needle that always points north.

They had twenty minutes to practice using their compass. After that, they would be on their own. Each group was assigned a teaching assistant, but that person could help only in case of an emergency.

On Team #1, Dom and Iona were itching to get started. They had little patience for practicing as they waited for Ms. Allport to hand out the secret envelope that contained their target destination. The team, rounded out by Serena and Caleb, knew that if they could get there first, retrieve the red flag, and return to the mess hall before anyone else, they would win an ice cream cake made by the camp's chef. They wanted that ice cream cake!

Iona sported one of her favorite t-shirts. It read, "I may look like I'm listening, but I'm really waiting to talk." She ran through a list of flavors she wished the cake would be. "I hope it's butter brickle. I really love those candy pieces. Ooh, or chocolate chip cookie dough! That would be awesome. Or cookies and cream. You can't beat cookies and cream. We just have to win."

Dom replied, "No doubt about it. We're going to win."

Iona continued listing off ice cream flavors as Ms. Allport finished the instructions. "One last thing before I provide you with your location and set you free. I thought you might like to know that in the event of an emergency, you can create your own compass. You know that a magnetized needle points north. So, all you need to do is magnetize a needle. A sewing needle, metal wire, or clasp from an earring would do the job. Simply rub the positive end of a magnet up the needle about 40 times then place it on a leaf and set the leaf on some water. And there you have it: a homemade wilderness compass."

Whether or not they needed a homemade compass, Caleb planned to make one someday. How fascinating!

"Okay, everyone. Practice time is over," Ms. Allport announced. She then provided each group with a secret envelope containing a map of Camp Discovery. Each map was marked with a green dot that represented their current location and a large red X designating the location of their red flag.

Dom stood ready with one foot in front of him as if he were about to begin a race. "You may start any time," said Ms. Allport. "Good luck, everyone."

Dom snatched the map. "Follow me!"

"The Eagle has landed!" Iona cheered. "I'm with ya, Dom."

Caleb and Serena didn't move.

"Come on, you two," Dom directed. "What are you waiting for?"

"We don't even know where we're going. How do you know which direction to head?" Caleb asked.

"I looked at the map and I can see where we're supposed to go. We'll figure it out on the way."

"Maybe we should all talk this over," Serena suggested. "Nobody else has left yet, so we have time to talk about it before we leave."

Caleb chimed in. "I think we need a plan. We were given a compass for a reason. We know our current location. We know our target destination. We need to line up the edge of the baseplate between these two points, turn the dial on the compass to line up with true north, and then head in the direction of the travel arrow."

"Line up the what with the what?" Dom asked. "Forget it, I'm going. Follow me if you like."

Turning to Caleb, Serena said, "I think we should go with him. We're supposed to stay together. And we're not going to accomplish anything if we're arguing."

"But, we..." Caleb gasped. "Fine. This is going to be a disaster."

"First to leave!!!" Iona cheered. "We are soooo getting that ice cream cake. I hope it's chocolate chip cookie dough. Did I mention I like cookie dough?"

Dom charged onward, occasionally glancing at the map. The compass bounced along in his front pocket.

Along the way, Iona pointed out blooming flowers and tree buds heeding the calls of spring. A fire lookout tower in the distance stood guard over the forest. At one point, Iona insisted the group stop to watch a pair of chipmunks chasing after each other and bickering in high-pitched squeaks. "You don't see that every day," she laughed.

They soon passed a shed near a baseball diamond. Beside the shed, the groundskeeper was planting flowers. Iona called out to him, "Looks pretty sweet, dude!"

He glanced at the group then returned to his work.

Serena noticed that Caleb was getting increasingly frustrated. She walked beside him. "Don't worry. We'll figure it out."

"Not if we don't use the compass and the map."

Serena tried to pacify Caleb. "Sometimes it's better to remain quiet than to fight."

A few minutes later, Dom halted to look at the map. He seemed confused as he glanced around the forest. "I think this map is wrong."

Iona interjected, "I'm sure it's right. Maybe you're just holding it wrong."

"Okay, that's it," Caleb declared. "We are not going anywhere until we make a plan. We are going to sit down on that log, study this map, set up the compass, and do this the right way."

Dom looked puzzled. "Well, if you knew the right way, why didn't you tell us before we started?"

Caleb put his palm on his forehead.

"Whoa!" said Iona. "I have literally never seen anyone do the facepalm emoji. Like ever."

"Maybe we should all just take a breath and relax," Serena offered. "Remember, we are one team."

Caleb studied the map for two minutes, which felt like forever for Dom and Iona. Then, another two minutes. Then another. He wanted to be certain his plan was correct. Finally, he said, "I know where we're going. Let's head in this direction."

Now Dom was annoyed. After that long delay, he had all but given up hope they would win. What was the point in hurrying now? Then Iona pointed. "There it is! I see it. I see the red flag!"

She ran over and untied it from the branch. "Let's go. Now we just have to reverse our course and boom, ice cream cake!"

"Not so fast," Caleb interrupted. "I don't believe we took the best route here. We need to use the compass to find our way back. That is the point of this assignment, after all."

Dom brought his hand to his forehead. "Whoa!" exclaimed Iona. "It's a double facepalm emoji day. This has to be a Guinness World Record!"

The group wound their way back to the starting location in relative silence. At one point, Dom grumbled to the teaching assistant, "You know, there's an app for this. It's called GPS."

The teaching assistant, trying to contain her amusement, just smiled.

Before they could see the mess hall, they heard it. Based on the volume of chatter, they could tell that not everyone had returned, but the news was not good. Other teams had beaten them to the prize. A frowning Iona turned to her teammates. "I really wanted that ice cream. I think I can actually smell it. I'm pretty sure it's cookies and cream." She sighed. "But no worries. We'll win next time. And hey, at least we're not last."

Dom begged to differ. He kicked a rock into the bushes and pretended it didn't hurt. "Ooooh, good thing we had a *plaaaan*."

Serena, struggling to act unfazed, turned away from her group. Caleb's only regret was not doing the exercise right from the start. If only Dom had listened, Caleb thought.

CHAPTER FOUR

Following the ever-popular pizza night, everyone made their way to the amphitheater. Once again, the groundskeeper, not one to change a proven method, had lit a lattice fire. The students arranged themselves on the wooden benches, and even the teaching assistants joined in despite having the night off.

Mr. Marston perched his stool near the fire. "When we left off, the representatives from the four kingdoms introduced themselves to the Chameleon Ambassador. You may recall that we learned a little bit about Nightowl, Dovetail, Eagleye, and Parrotfeather. They were dispatched to Chamelia because their people needed help. Tonight, I will begin by telling you about the crises that faced the four bird kingdoms of Aviara."

Throughout the history of the Owl Kingdom, the people constructed sturdy buildings that could withstand even the windiest of storms. The design and strength of their homes were the envy of the other kingdoms. In recent years, storms had been getting worse, causing many homes in the Dove, Parrot, and Eagle Kingdoms to sustain significant damage and even collapse. These kingdoms needed the Owl's scientific and architectural knowledge to better predict storms and erect sturdier buildings.

Many people in the Dove Kingdom became healers for both the body and the mind. They cared about living beings and became quite skilled at rehabilitating people and animals from injuries and diseases. They also became counselors to help people through difficult times. Over the past few winters, a mysterious disease had spread across Aviara, and only the Doves had found a way to cure it. People throughout the continent needed their compassion and medical wisdom.

For centuries, the Eagle Kingdom had shown great strength and military discipline. They stood boldly against the bordering Kingdom of Vultura, which had never dared challenge the confident Eagles. But recently, the Vulturans had begun to test the more vulnerable Parrot, Dove, and Owl Kingdoms.

Like the vultures they observed, the Vulturans preyed on the weaknesses of others. The Vulturan culture, lacking in joy, knew only fear and hostility. They cared only about themselves. They didn't know how to build, only how to destroy. They didn't know how to heal, only how to hurt others with their words and actions. With Aviara overwhelmed by crises, the Vulturans recognized an opportunity to steal the possessions and land of the Parrot, Owl, and Dove Kingdoms. Vulturan raids into Aviara spread fear across the continent.

The Parrots had always maintained a positive spirit when faced with tremendous challenges. They lived by the motto, "Nothing great has ever been accomplished with negativity." With the threat of a Vulturan invasion, increasingly dangerous storms, and a mysterious disease, the Eagles, Owls, and Doves felt hopeless. The continent needed Parrot optimism more than ever.

The four emissaries shared the challenges facing their kingdoms, and the Chameleon Ambassador summarized them in response. "If I am hearing you correctly, you face crises of knowledge, health, security, and spirit in Aviara. You notice that Chameleons live in harmony by practicing the ways of each of your kingdoms. It is our understanding that you view us as a model for what you may create for the continent.

"Very accurate summary," Nightowl acknowledged.

"We would love to help you, but our assistance is not required."

"What are you talking about?" Eagleye snapped. "You just heard about the illnesses sweeping our nations, the storms destroying our homes, and the Vulturans threatening our safety. People are losing faith. How can you say that your help is 'not required?'"

"The Chameleons are the eyes of the forest. We see all, but are rarely seen. We listen, but are rarely heard. We observed you on your travels here, and our help is not needed."

"Wait. Hold on," Eagleye screeched. "You were watching us?"

"That's what she took away from the Ambassador's comments?" Parrotfeather whispered to Dovetail.

The Ambassador smirked knowingly. "That's what we do. We watch. We listen. We learn."

"I don't understand," Dovetail said. "Can you share why you are not willing to work with our four kingdoms? Our situation grows worse every day.

We need to learn how to work together just as you do in Chamelia. Won't you please share what you have learned?"

Mr. Marston stood from his stool. "I'm going to stop here and rewind our story just a bit. Let's revisit the four emissaries after they walked together for several hours. Maybe that will reveal why the Ambassador is unwilling to help."

When the four emissaries arrived at the place where they thought the Chameleon Ambassador would be waiting, instead they found four wooden statues. Each contained a scroll bound by a ribbon. Perched atop a hand-carved, wooden mountain sat an Eagle with an outstretched wing. Resting upon the wing, Eagleye found a scroll wrapped in a red ribbon. She slid the ribbon off the ancient parchment without untying it and unfurled the paper. She read the instructions printed in big bold letters. Eagleye knew exactly what to do.

Nightowl's message was nestled inside a statue of a tree. From the hollow, a meticulously carved owl stared into her eyes. Clasped in its talons was a scroll tied with a blue ribbon. Nightowl examined the artistry of the craftsmanship before carefully removing the scroll. After untying the ribbon and setting it aside, Nightowl sat silently as she pondered its words.

Parrotfeather was dazzled by his statue, which was the only painted one. Three red, green, and blue parrots held glasses high in the air, clinking them together in celebration. A scroll tied with a bright yellow ribbon protruded from one of the mugs. Parrotfeather opened it hastily and shimmered with enthusiasm after reading the contents.

Nightowl wondered what could be that exciting.

Dovetail was the last to retrieve a scroll. He was too busy enjoying the reactions of the others as they read their instructions. Eagleye looked determined. Nightowl appeared thoughtful. And Parrotfeather was animated as usual. Dovetail's heart melted when he saw a wooden nest housing a family of doves. At the center, a scroll tied with a green ribbon waited for him. He opened it feeling the burden of responsibility on his shoulders. The words within mattered not just to Dovetail but to his fellow emissaries and all Aviarans. Dovetail read the message several times then re-tied the scroll and placed it back where he found it.

Once Eagleye and Parrotfeather saw that

everyone had retrieved their messages, they were eager to go.

"Adventure awaits!" Parrotfeather announced.

"Follow my lead," Eagleye directed.

"One moment please," Nightowl requested. "Before we leave, I think it would be wise to examine the quests of those who have come before us. Our ancestors made the journey we are about to undertake many times."

Nightowl went into vivid detail about the first meeting...and the second...and the third. By the fourth meeting, Eagleye couldn't take it anymore. "That's it for me. I'm leaving. Follow me."

"But we haven't reviewed all their travels. Shouldn't we learn from the past so we don't make their same mistakes?" Nightowl's question didn't turn any of the three backs venturing farther into the Nest.

Eagleye took control. "I'll get us there. Again, it's not complicated. We follow this path and we find the Chameleons."

Nightowl disagreed. "But this path splits off into many other paths. How will we know which ones to take?"

"When we get there, we'll decide."

This all made Dovetail uneasy, but he didn't want to upset the others. He kept his thoughts and feelings to himself.

The group proceeded onwards. At every fork in the path, Eagleye selected a direction without hesitation, as if she had undertaken this quest many times before.

Dovetail grew increasingly uncomfortable. He occasionally shared his concerns with Parrotfeather, who insisted that Dovetail needn't worry. Everything would work out, because in his words, "It always does."

After walking for several hours, the group heard footsteps shuffling along on the path ahead. Rounding the turn, they saw an old man holding a walking stick approach with difficulty. He coughed several times and told the four emissaries to stay back, warning them that he wasn't feeling well.

Eagleye, Nightowl, and Parrotfeather stepped off the path to let the old man pass, but Dovetail did not move. He retrieved a green silk mask from his pocket and secured it over his mouth and nose. He then reached into his pack for a pair of gloves. "What seems to be ailing you?" he asked the weary traveler.

The old man described his symptoms, and Dovetail politely asked him to sit on a stump. The emissary from the Dove Kingdom told him that he would return shortly. Minutes later, he emerged from the forest carrying leaves from several plants. The group watched in curiosity as he ground them to a powder and then stirred them into the old man's water canteen. Dovetail told him to drink the mixture daily and demonstrated how to identify and compile the leafy ingredients. "In a few days, you'll feel restored," said Dovetail with a modest bow. "This is an old family remedy."

Nightowl had recorded each ingredient in her notebook and sketched the leaves. Eagleye was certain she could memorize each step. Parrotfeather planned to copy Nightowl's notes later.

After the man left, Dovetail recommended that the emissaries wash their hands to avoid getting sick. They did so willingly and continued on their way.

After arriving at their campsite, they spent the night in relative silence, speaking only when necessary—perhaps because Parrotfeather had fallen asleep from exhaustion.

The next morning, Nightowl could remain silent no more. Just before setting off, she stated her concerns. "I believe we have lost our way. We did not learn from those who have come before us, and we don't have a plan."

Dovetail politely waited for Nightowl to finish. "I believe I can help," he offered.

With an explosion of excitement, the rejuvenated Parrotfeather announced, "I know what to do!"

Nightowl tried to contain the Parrot emissary, but he was so excited about his idea that everyone just followed along, including Eagleye.

What happened next did not sit well with Nightowl. Parrotfeather hung a sharp right and abandoned the well-traveled path, heading deep into the woods. Parrotfeather seemed to bounce along as he shared story after story of his previous adventures with friends. One story led right into the next, barely giving anyone else the chance to speak or interject thoughts about where they were headed.

After bushwhacking like this for a while, Parrotfeather suddenly stopped. He looked to his right, then to his left. He stood on his tippy toes trying to look over the hill in front of them. He turned around and looked suspectly at the branches they'd disturbed to get there. "Ya know, I'm not positive this is right."

Eagleye's and Nightowl's jaws dropped. The Eagle emissary fumed. "What do you mean that you are not positive this is right?"

Without thinking, Dovetail stepped between Eagleye and Parrotfeather and said, "We are all working towards the same objective. We are here to help our people. All of our people. I have an idea if you would like to hear it."

Nobody replied. Dovetail took a deep breath for everyone to hear, as if willing them to do the same, then began. "I believe that if we follow the river, it will lead us to a pair of large boulders. There will be a path that lies between them. That path will lead us directly to the Chameleon Ambassador who is awaiting our arrival."

"Those are oddly specific instructions," noted Nightowl. "How do you know this?"

"The scroll told me," replied the Dove representative.

"Whoa, hold on," Eagleye said. "You knew how to get there and didn't tell us?"

"Well, we all had instructions. In the beginning, Nightowl wanted to review past expeditions, and I didn't want to interrupt. Then, you seemed so confident that I didn't wish to disagree with you. Then Parrotfeather was so delighted to leave the path, who was I to disagree?"

Nightowl just shook her head. "So you knew how to get there this entire time but didn't say anything?"

"I tried to, but nobody would listen," Dovetail said. "And this is the exact reason why I didn't want to start bossing everyone around. I didn't want us to argue."

"How about this," Nightowl suggested. "We all sit down in that clearing over there, review each of our instructions, and then create a plan."

"I suppose I could use a break anyway," Eagleye conceded. "But we can't take long. It looks like a storm is rolling in."

The group reviewed the contents of their scrolls. They mapped out their path forward and picked a campsite for the second evening of their journey. They felt confident they were now on the right path.

When they arrived at the campsite, a gentle

mist filled the air. The wind had picked up, heralding a storm. As they set up their tents, Nightowl explained how to secure their shelters against the incoming weather with steel stakes his people forged in the Owl Kingdom. The wind howled through the night, but their tents stood strong.

They prepared a quick breakfast, packed up their gear, and were on their way. Once again, they hiked with little conversation. They had just climbed over a large hill when Eagleye held her right arm high at a right angle, commanding her fellow travelers to a halt. She placed a finger to her lips indicating they should remain silent.

That's when they saw it. Coiled in the center of the path was a snake. Its head swayed side to side as if scanning for prey.

Eagleye turned to the other three emissaries and said, "Stand tall. Look directly into his eyes. Hold the intention that he is no match for you."

Nightowl, Dovetail, and Parrotfeather did their best to comply.

Eagleye then faced the snake and said with a booming voice, "We mean you no harm. Be on your way."

At first, the snake didn't budge. Eagleye took a step closer and said even louder, "We mean you no harm. Leave!"

The snake slithered into the woods, and the group breathed a collective sigh of relief. They were happy that Eagleye knew what to do. The group remained alert for predators the rest of the journey.

The emissaries followed the winding river per Dovetail's instructions. Parrotfeather marveled at the green hills that rolled like ocean waves. A few hours before they arrived to meet the Chameleon Ambassador, Parrotfeather spoke. "I don't know about any of you, but I'm excited to be here. We are about to meet a real-life Chameleon. I've never met one before and I can't wait. Have any of you?"

They all shook their heads no.

"We have been given a great responsibility by our people. I'm proud to have been chosen, and I'm guessing all of you are too. Is that right?"

They all nodded.

"Instead of finishing out this trip with gloomy faces, how about we spend the rest of our time sharing stories about our homelands? I, for one, would like to learn about each of your kingdoms. Who's in?"

Dovetail said, "I would like that."

They each told stories about their families and the land in which they were raised. When they rounded the final turn, they were chatting joyfully when they saw the Chameleon Ambassador in her wooden chair.

Mr. Marston left a long silence then turned to the students and said, "It seems like our four emissaries faced some interesting challenges of their own as they traveled together. Before we return to our story, I want to check in with all of you. How are the four emissaries doing?"

"I like how they became friends," Iona said.

"Yeah, but in the beginning of their trip, they didn't get along so well," Dom called out.

"I can't argue with you there, Dom," Mr. Marston replied. "And why not?"

Serena raised her hand. "They weren't listening to each other."

"That's for sure. Why else?" asked the teacher.

Caleb was next to speak. "They failed to use the information they had been given."

"Also true. They weren't communicating very well, and it made their journey more difficult than it had to be," Mr. Marston concluded. "Let's return to our story where the

Chameleon Ambassador has just told the emissaries that her assistance is not required. We'll pick it up from there…"

Dovetail spoke first. "Please Ambassador, you have to give us a chance. Our people need your help. If we can't figure out how to come together and support each other, many lives will be lost—in all of our kingdoms."

"We came all this way because we believe in you," Parrotfeather added. "We need to learn how to bring our people together so we can learn from each other."

The Ambassador gave an understanding nod.

Nightowl silently gathered her thoughts, then said to the Ambassador, "May I ask you a question?"

The Ambassador smiled. "Of course. Questions are a gateway to knowledge. You may ask anything you like, my Owl friend."

"Did we do something that offended you or the Chameleons? If so, we are unaware."

"You did not offend us. You just aren't ready for what we Chameleons have to share."

"Is there something we can do to get ready?" asked the Owl emissary.

The Ambassador remained still for a long time. Then, after taking several deep breaths, she looked into the eyes of each emissary, one by one. "You have traveled a great distance to get here and your people are in peril. Perhaps if I teach you the Chameleon Code, you will understand."

"What is the Chameleon Code?" Nightowl asked.

The Ambassador grinned. "The Chameleon Code contains four questions that are the foundation of all wisdom. They lead to an understanding so powerful, they would forever change the way you see each other and the world around you. They would allow you to solve any problem you face, no matter how challenging. But if I agree to share our sacred code with you, you must agree to bring this wisdom back to your people to teach it to everyone. You must pass it down from generation to generation. Only then will I share the questions that make up the Chameleon Code. Only then will you be able to help your people. All of your people. Do you agree to my terms?"

One by one, they nodded in agreement. "Then let us begin. Have a seat, my weary travelers."

The four emissaries made themselves comfortable in the chairs provided by the Ambassador who, composing herself to lead an adventure inward, took measure of each pupil.

"Question number one of the Chameleon Code should be easy for you, but it is not understood by most. In fact, the first question may be the most powerful question we can ask ourselves."

"So what is it?" Eagleye asked impatiently.

"Which bird am I?" said the Ambassador.

"What do you mean?" Eagleye replied.

"Which bird kingdom do you hail from?" clarified the Ambassador.

"That's it?" Eagleye snapped.

"But everyone knows that," Parrotfeather shrugged. "I am from the Parrot Kingdom. Dovetail is from the Dove Kingdom. Nightowl..."

The Ambassador held up her hand. "This was not always so. In the old times, Aviara was one nation. Everyone lived together in harmony. But as the population grew and the four kingdoms took on their own personalities, they struggled to understand each other. They found it difficult to communicate with one another and, eventually, they stopped trying."

The emissaries nodded in agreement. They knew this was their great challenge: to work together to overcome the crises facing Aviara.

Mr. Marston scanned the group. "Last night, you didn't realize it, but you were answering the Ambassador's first question, 'Which bird am I?' But before we continue with our story, we have a tasty activity for you. On the tables behind you, there is a warm batch of sugar cookies. Let's give the teaching assistants a round of applause for making them for you."

Everyone applauded gratefully. Iona's hearty clapping seemed to fill the amphitheater with echoes. Dom, not to be outdone, tried to clap even louder.

"Over here, you will find different colored tubes of frosting, sprinkles, chocolate chips, and more. You will notice that the cookies are in the shapes of eagles, parrots, doves, and owls."

Just before Mr. Marston was about to release everyone to decorate the cookies, Iona called out with a sarcastic grin, "So you're feeding us bird food?"

"I suppose we are," laughed the teacher. "Enjoy your bird food, everyone."

After the break, the students returned to their seats. As they settled in, Mr. Marston explained that the first question,

"Which bird am I?" is based on the age-old question, "Who am I?" He told them that people who truly know themselves are the happiest and most successful people. They get along with others and, when it's time, they find a path in life that allows them to shine. "Let's get back to our story though. The Ambassador is about to reveal the second question of the Chameleon Code."

Nightowl began, "So you shared the first question, 'Which Bird are You?' What is the second question?"

The Ambassador continued, "While the first question was easy for you since you come from one of four bird kingdoms, you struggled with the second question during your journey here."

Dovetail's thoughtful look prompted the Ambassador to ask him, "Do you have an idea of what the second question might be?"

"I was wondering if it has to do with how we treated each other. We didn't do so well on the first part of our time together."

"Not quite, but we'll get to that later. Before I answer, tell me about your journey here. Begin after you met at the ancestral meeting place," the Ambassador requested.

"We succeeded," Eagleye said. "We're here, aren't we?"

"I am more concerned with how you behaved than the fact that you arrived."

They considered the question until Parrotfeather broke the silence. "I guess I was being my Parrot self. I talk a lot and that's what I did."

"And I took charge," Eagleye added.

"Yes, but did you both do so in the best way possible?"

Eagleye and Parrotfeather shrugged.

The Ambassador paused to give her next words the respect they deserved. "The second question of the Chameleon Code is, 'Is my bird at its best?'"

Parrotfeather was about to speak when the Ambassador raised her hand. "Why did you get lost on your way here?"

"How did you know we got lost? And actually, we weren't lost. We just didn't take the most direct route," Eagleye explained.

The Ambassador grinned knowingly "As I told you, Chameleons are the eyes of the forest. We see all but are rarely seen."

Eagleye didn't like that answer, but she allowed the Ambassador to continue.

"Let me rephrase that question just a bit. What did each of you do or not do that led to your difficulty in getting here? After all, each of your scrolls contained a part of your directions. And I know because I wrote them. Four parts to one set of instructions. Four kingdoms. One continent. One people. One map."

The Ambassador let her words sink in, then continued, "Your actions showed that you were not being your best selves. You see, we all have our own way of being. And when we are at our best, we shine brightly. But sometimes, we let our strengths shine too brightly and they become our weaknesses. We have a saying among the Chameleons that makes us think about the second question of the Chameleon Code: Did you shine your light just right or too bright?"

Nightowl scrunched his eyebrows together in thought. "Can you explain what you mean by shining our light too bright?"

"When your bird is at its best, you build long-lasting friendships and accomplish incredible things. But if you shine your light too brightly, you can upset the people in your life and not achieve your goals."

"I see," Nightowl acknowledged. "If we use our strengths, they work for us. But if we overuse them, they work against us."

"Perfectly stated," replied the Ambassador. "Allow me to demonstrate. Eagleye, as an Eagle, you are confident and make things happen. You make quick decisions and easily take charge of a situation. Can you tell us what your scroll told you to do?"

"Sure. It said, 'Follow the Eagles.'"

"How did you interpret that?" the Ambassador asked.

"Easy. I'm an Eagle. Everyone should follow me."

"Fascinating. Did you notice that at the outset of your journey there were 12 eagles' nests that formed a line pointing directly to where we now sit?"

"Ummm...I didn't see that."

"So instead of following the eagle nests, what did you do?"

"I took charge and told everyone to follow me! That's what I always do," Eagleye replied. "But as I think about it now, I wasn't listening. I saw myself as the leader, and leaders tell people what to do."

"Sometimes leaders tell people what to do," said the Ambassador, "but great leaders also listen to those around them. They make decisions after gathering information, ideas, and opinions."

"I see," Eagleye said. "If I were shining my light just right, I would have been a leader who collaborated with my fellow emissaries rather than boss them around. I shined my Eagle light too brightly."

"Exactly," confirmed the Ambassador. "Let's see what the rest of you were told. Dovetail, what did your scroll say?"

As usual, he took a deep breath before speaking. "I was provided with specific directions and landmarks."

"Did you share this information with everyone?" asked the Ambassador.

"Yes. Well, not at first."

"Why not?" the Ambassador wondered.

"I was trying to be respectful. Eagleye seemed certain about where we should begin. Then Parrotfeather was so excited about his ideas, I didn't want to disagree with him."

"Because harmony is important to you?"

"Oh yes, very important. I figured we wouldn't

get anywhere if we were arguing."

"So, rather than speak up, which would have helped the group, you chose to maintain harmony over providing the information you were given. You didn't speak up because you didn't want to upset others."

"I suppose that's what I did," the Dove admitted.

"You wanted to avoid conflict, which can be a good thing, but you shined your light so brightly that you withheld valuable information for fear of upsetting others."

"I can see that now," Dovetail said. "I guess that too much of a good thing is not a good thing."

"Beautiful," said the Ambassador. "Nightowl, will you share what your scroll said?"

"Sure. It said, 'Walk in the footsteps of those who have come before you. The wisdom of past journeys reveals the path for this one.'"

"And so, you sought to review the fine details of all past journeys."

"Yes, I did. I didn't want to miss anything."

"But in doing so, you went into so much detail, shining your light so brightly, you blinded others with too much information. And those details overwhelmed and frustrated your traveling companions."

"So, details are important," reflected Nightowl, "but too much detail can be confusing to others."

"Precisely!" exclaimed the Ambassador.

"I suppose I'm next," said Parrotfeather. "Uh oh."

"Why uh oh?"

"I think I blinded everyone! Is anyone here seeing spots?"

"Explain."

"Well, my scroll told me to be creative and forge my own path and bring my spirit to the journey. So I did. I figured that if we left the path, we could find our way. Things always work out, so I assumed we'd get here eventually. And along the way, we could enjoy the trip. I even added some stories to pass the time."

"Lots of stories," Eagleye interjected.

"Okay, lots of stories. But hey, I'm a storyteller. My people are storytellers. That's what we do."

"And that is a wonderful thing," the Ambassador replied. "But sometimes you have to give others the chance to speak. You have to let others shine their light. If you shine your light too brightly, others remain in the dark."

"Ooh, that's going to be a hard one," Parrotfeather laughed.

"You see, everyone, the second question, 'Is my bird at its best?' means that you have to use your strengths but not overuse them. Shine your light brightly but not so brightly that it blinds others from seeing your greatness."

The Ambassador looked over her shoulder and saw a red and yellow sky behind her. She turned to the group and said, "The sun is beginning to set. I can see that you understand the second question of the Chameleon Code. Let's make a fire and enjoy a meal together. Tonight, we'll get to know each other better. Tomorrow, we can continue the conversation."

Mr. Marston turned to watch the fire for a moment. When he turned to look at the students, he said, "Before we call it a night, I want to take a few minutes to reflect on your experience from earlier today."

The students had a lively discussion about their orienteering adventure. Dom thought about how he had taken charge just like Eagleye and how that didn't serve the group. He realized that he told everyone what to do without listening to the rest of the team.

Caleb pondered how, just like Nightowl, he got caught up in the details and how that slowed their progress. He needed to share important information but not let that become more important than the goal.

Iona reflected on how she was so excited to make their experience fun, she lost sight of the goal. She also recognized that she talked so much, she didn't give others the chance to share their stories.

And Serena related to Dovetail's quiet need for harmony and how that ultimately didn't serve the team. She realized that her ideas were important and that it's okay to speak up and let her thoughts and opinions be known.

After a great talk, everyone was ready to head back to the cabins. Mr. Marston closed by saying, "Get a good night's sleep everyone. Tomorrow is a big day!"

CHAPTER FIVE

The students awakened to a dark, troubled sky. Fortunately, it wasn't raining yet. Unfortunately, the breakfast wasn't much better than the weather. The students had a choice between cereal from tiny cardboard boxes that filled only half a small bowl—or dry pancakes—all to be washed down with watery orange juice. It wasn't a great start to the day.

The campers cleaned up from the meal, while the teaching assistants prepared the mess hall for the first activity. They folded the tables and wheeled them to the back of the mess hall, leaving four of them open along the walls.

Ms. Allport called the group to attention to share Wednesday's agenda. "Gather round, Galen 5th graders. This afternoon, we will be conducting soil and water experiments. Right now, I want you to imagine you are all a group of paleontologists. That means you study the history of life on Earth by examining fossils. You are on an expedition that is taking place right here in the mess hall. You've been working hard for weeks and just made an incredible discovery. You have found an ancient cave that has never been seen by human eyes. We are standing inside that cave right now. Put on your imagination hats and tell me what you see."

Celeb replied, "It's dark."

"That it is. Good thing we brought lights," she winked.

Iona called out, "I see a lot of spiky things coming up from the ground and down from the ceiling."

"Excellent. Stalagmites are the mounds rising up from the cave floor. Stalactites are hanging like icicles from above. What else?"

Serena added, "There's a small waterfall. It's really peaceful."

"Wonderful. I love your creativity. I'll tell you what else I see," Ms. Allport said. "In this corner, I see ancient dinosaur eggs. They can help us learn amazing things about these extinct creatures. The eggs are so delicate, we cannot touch them. The oils from our skin would cause permanent damage. Your challenge is to move the eggs from the starting point—this rope that crosses the mess hall floor—to the ending point, which is that rope over there where the cafeteria line begins."

Iona could barely contain her excitement. She turned to the person next to her—it didn't matter who!—and said, "Ooh, I love an adventure."

Ms. Allport was about to ask Iona to remain silent while she was speaking, but then she read Iona's t-shirt: "You can move my seat, but I'm still going to talk to the person next to me." Shushing her would be a waste of time.

The teacher continued, "Each team will be given a single marble. That marble represents a dinosaur egg. We've got a lot of rules, so bear with me."

Dom turned to Caleb. "I hate rules."

Caleb, puzzled by Dom's reaction, raised his hand and asked, "Should we write them down?"

Knowing Caleb, Ms. Allport couldn't help grinning. "That will not be necessary. I will provide a written copy of the rules when I'm done so you can review them with your team."

Serena whispered to Caleb, "That was a good question. I appreciate your Owlness."

"Here are the rules. As you attempt to move the marble, you cannot touch it. The only time you can touch the marble is before the starting line and after the finishing line. Marbles cannot be thrown and cannot touch the floor. If a marble is dropped or touched by anyone on the team, you must return the marble to the starting line and begin again. You cannot attach the marble to anything, and it must continually move forward on your device, which you will build."

"What can we build the device out of?" Caleb asked.

"You may use anything from nature you find outside. And when I say 'nature,' it must be a part of nature, like a branch or stone, not a hose or plank of wood that happens to be in nature. Branches cannot be longer than three feet long, so each team will be issued a tape measure to check the size. You will also receive a roll of masking tape to help construct your device."

Dom turned back to Caleb and said, "She wasn't kidding about a lot of rules. Did you catch all that?"

"I think so, but don't worry. We are getting printed instructions."

The students were assigned to teams and got ready for action. Serena, Dom, Iona, and Caleb were joined by four others from one of the previous day's orienteering groups.

The teaching assistants distributed the supplies. Dom reached out his hand for the marble as Caleb retrieved the tape measure and tape.

"Okay everyone, you have fifteen minutes to gather items from outside. It looks like it's going to rain soon, so collect your materials quickly. After that, you will have thirty minutes to construct a device. We need to get these dinosaur eggs out of the cave! Your time to gather building materials starts…" she paused to look at her watch and then announced, "Now!"

As the students filed towards the door, Caleb called to his teammates. "Before we begin, do you think we should talk about what we are trying to find?"

After the orienteering disaster, Dom and Iona figured they should listen to what Caleb had to say. "I'm thinking we need a bunch of long sticks. Maybe we could use some flat stones and a few big leaves. What does everyone else think?"

The rest of the team thought that sounded good and off they went. With thunder booming and the sky turning darker by the minute, they gathered a pile of branches along with an assortment of pinecones and long strips of bark from a birch tree. Caleb reminded his teammates that branches, not bark, were limited to three feet.

There was a flurry of activity near the mess hall, though some students wandered farther away as time passed. A stormy mist settled around them. They could barely see the mess hall let alone the nearby forest. Most of the students had returned to the mess hall with one notable exception. With seconds to spare, Iona burst through the door panting. She was using the bottom of her shirt as a basket to carry several brown-and-white-striped feathers, brightly colored leaves, a piece of moss, a few acorns, and some wildflowers. She triumphantly announced, "I'm not sure if these will help us, but they'll definitely look good."

"You found some really nice things," Serena said to a pleased Iona.

"Thanks, Dovetail! I mean Serena," Iona winked.

Serena laughed and replied, "Sure thing, Parrotfeather."

Caleb carefully inspected each item, considering possible ways they could use them. Occasionally, he measured a stick to make sure it did not exceed the three-foot limit. He seemed particularly interested in several Y-shaped branches. "These will be very helpful," Caleb said quietly to himself.

Just as Ms. Allport announced that collection time had come to an end, a boom of thunder shook the mess hall, and heavy rain began to tap and eventually pound on the metal roof. "Well," she said, "that means it's time to build your devices for moving the dinosaur eggs. Those eggs aren't going to move themselves. Oh, and I forgot to mention that each team needs a name. Before we begin removing the eggs from the cave, you can share your team name with the rest of us."

Iona had five possible names in her head before anyone spoke. Serena thought of a name but wasn't sure if the group would like it. Caleb, who was thinking about the device, paused to question why a team name was even needed. Dom, remembering Eagleye's mistakes, realized that "Team Dom" wouldn't fly. Iona committed to working on their name while the rest of the team prepared to construct their device.

Ms. Allport continued, "You have a half hour to create your dinosaur egg mover. In this first round, the team that crosses the finish line first earns 100 points. Second team across gets 75. Third gets 50. And the last team to get their egg across the line will receive 25 points. Good luck, everyone. Remember, you have 30 minutes for construction and planning."

The students frantically began building their egg movers.

Dom grabbed the four longest branches and declared, "Here's what we should do. We press two sticks together like this." Dom demonstrated by holding the sticks tightly next to each other. "Then we put the marble between the sticks and let it roll down the middle. When it gets to the end of the first set of sticks, we transfer it to a second set held by two other people. We keep doing that all the way to the finish line. The challenge will be transferring the marble from one set of sticks to another, but I'm sure we can do it."

"We could totally pull that off!" Iona cheered.

"Great. Let's do it," Dom said.

"Ummm, I think that's a good first idea," Caleb said, "but maybe we should consider some other options too. We have lots of items that can be used in different ways. I suggest we explore what we can do with them."

Dom reassured the team, "I'm not telling everyone what to do. I'm just sharing my ideas."

"Remember when we learned about not shining our light too brightly? Well, bright light! Bright light!" Iona laughed.

"Okay, fine. I guess that sounded like I made the decision for all of us. Maybe that was a little too Eagle. What does everyone else think we should do?"

Caleb started to speak when Iona burst in. "How about we try it? We won't know if it works unless we give it a shot."

Caleb thought about how Parrotfeather got the group lost when they left the path, but realized they needed to do some testing anyway, so he agreed.

Dom grabbed the sticks and assigned them to various team members. As soon as they placed the marble on the sticks and started to roll it forward, the branches slightly parted and the marble fell to the floor.

"You have to keep the sticks together," Dom instructed. "Try it again."

The team tried again, and this time the marble rolled off the side of the sticks. They tried several more times, but the marble kept falling. "We need new people holding the sticks. You two," said Dom, pointing to two team members who were not part of the initial attempts. "Take the sticks and see if you can do it."

The same thing happened again.

"You have to focus," Dom insisted.

"We are focused," replied one of the team members.

Serena whispered to the team member Dom just corrected, "This is hard. That was a good try."

After several more attempts, it became clear that this strategy was not going to work. "I suggest we think about this for a minute," Caleb recommended. "If we tape the sticks together, I think that might help."

Serena looked ready to say something, but Iona couldn't

contain her thunderous excitement, "Oooh, I love that idea! Let's do it!"

Serena remembered how Dovetail struggled to speak up when doing so was important. She took a deep breath and said, "There are a bunch of people who haven't had the chance to speak yet. I feel like we should listen to their ideas before we try out this one."

"Sounds good to me," Iona said. "I'm sorry. I think my Parrot excitement is getting the best of me. I'm going to dim my light just a bit." She outstretched her arm and mimed lowering the brightness on a dial. "There, that's better."

The group deliberated. Caleb held up each item and asked for possible uses. The conversation led to some interesting ideas, including how they could use the Y-shaped branches and birch bark.

Dom was ready to get building so Caleb summarized. "Here's what we've got. We tape sticks together so they don't come apart. We place some leaves at the ends of the sticks. This will allow us to overlap them to help the marble roll more easily between each set of branches. We set the pairs of sticks into the V-part of two Y-shaped branches. We place birch bark along the sides to prevent the marble from sliding off. That about does it."

"And that's how Nightowl rolls!" exclaimed Iona.

Caleb tried to hide his satisfaction.

"We also talked about how we would take turns holding the sticks," Serena reminded the group.

"Oh yeah," Dom said. "We switch off holding the sticks because Serena wants everyone to get a chance to move the marble."

"Aaaaaaand," Iona said suggestively.

"And Parrotfeather over here wants to add some feathers and flowers to the sides of the sticks to make them look awesome," Dom laughed. "Does that capture it?"

Several team members nodded and Dom accepted that as agreement. They practiced for a few more minutes until Ms. Allport declared it was time to begin. She lifted the whistle from around her neck and said, "When I blow this whistle, you can start. We will not stop until all groups have saved their dinosaur eggs. Get ready. We start transporting dinosaur eggs in one minute."

Everyone carried their supplies to the starting line. When everyone was in place and ready, Ms. Allport turned to Caleb, Serena, Iona, and Dom's group and asked, "What is your team name?"

Iona, clearly pleased with her idea, announced, "We're the Karma Chameleons."

"Very nice."

Ms. Allport turned to the second team and asked for their name. On a count of three, the group responded in harmony,

"We're the Galeontologists."

"I see what you did there," smiled the teacher.

The final two teams reported their names as the Dino Blasters and the Wingdings. It was time to move the eggs to safety.

"Remember, first place gets 100 points, then 75, 50, and 25. On three. One. Two. Three. Go!" She blew the whistle and the formerly quiet room broke into frenzied activity. Students could barely hear each other, and the volume rose as they shouted instructions to fellow team members. Plans that made sense during the quiet of their practice period were falling apart as marbles bounced off the floor.

The Dino Blasters got off to a great start. They made it halfway to the finish line when their marble slid off the branches they had taped together. This group used a slightly different method than the Karma Chameleons. Instead of two branches, they used three. This allowed them to position the outside branches higher than the middle branch, thus creating a track for the marble to roll in. They were doing well until they angled the contraption downward a little too steeply, causing the marble to gain too much speed and fall to the floor.

The Wingdings could barely move the marble past the starting line without losing it. Several of their team members were barking out opposite commands.

"Hurry up. The other teams are winning!" said one voice.

"Slow down. You're going to drop it!" shouted another. Too many Eagles over there, thought Caleb.

The Galeontologists were moving slowly, but so far, they didn't have any mishaps. Their strategy seemed to be "slow and steady wins the race"—and it was working. They had designated one person to give instructions to the team, and everyone seemed to be listening and following directions as they were given.

The Karma Chameleons were doing well. Caleb, Serena, and two other team members were holding two Y-shaped sticks vertically. Lying horizontally in the center of the Y were the two branches bound together with tape. Dom provided instructions on how to move, and Iona cheered on her teammates. At one point, the device angled to the side and the marble jumped over the birch bark and fell to the ground.

With enthusiasm, Iona reassured her team. "That's okay. We're fine. Let's restart and get it next time!"

The Wingdings and Dino Blasters were having some difficulty. It was coming down to the Galeontologists and the Karma Chameleons.

With Iona cheering, "Karma, Karma, Karma, Karma, Karma Chameleons!" her team kept the positive energy flowing.

The Galeontologists were moving slowly but getting close to the finishing rope. With the Karma Chameleons on their heels, the Galeontologists crossed the finish line just ahead of Caleb, Serena, Dom, Iona, and their teammates.

The activity continued until the Dino Blasters crossed the finish line, followed several minutes later by the Wingdings. Ms. Allport walked to the center of the room and faced the groups now on the other side of the mess hall.

"You did it! You saved the dinosaur eggs! I'm very impressed with all of you. Who's ready for round two?"

Everyone's hands went up, except for a few from the Wingdings, who were clearly frustrated.

"In this round, each team will receive ten marbles. The same points apply for first, second, third, and fourth places. You will have seven minutes to get as many marbles across the finish line as possible. One extra rule: You may not tape the marbles together."

"Darn," Iona muttered, wondering how Ms. Allport knew what she was thinking.

"You have ten minutes for planning, so get started."

The word "planning" spurred Caleb to start the discussion. "I think our strategy worked well, but with ten marbles, we might want to change how we do this."

"What are you thinking?" Dom asked.

"I think we have two options. Either we get one marble across at a time and then go back for more, or we try to get them all across at once."

Caleb thought for a moment longer then added, "Or, I suppose we can try to get two marbles across at a time and then go back for more. Or maybe three. Or four. Or maybe two trips of five. I guess we have a lot of options."

Iona stared into Caleb's eyes, prompting him to say, "Bright light. Bright light. I get it."

Dom took charge. "How about we try moving all ten at once and see what happens?"

"Testing out a strategy makes sense to me," Caleb agreed.

The group tried all ten at once but discovered that it was just too many to manage. They tried five and that seemed like too many as well. When they attempted to move three marbles, they easily transferred all three from one set of sticks to the next.

Just as Caleb was summarizing their plan of moving three marbles from one set of sticks to another, Iona started jumping up and down. "I got it! I got it! I know I'm being a Parrot, but this is a good idea."

"We figured you had an idea," Dom said plainly. "What is it? We don't have much time."

"What if we create two more sets of branches? We can have three or four marbles on each set of sticks at a time. That would give us an extra set to run in front of the others and keep us moving forward."

"This sounds complicated to coordinate," Caleb worried,

"but it's worth a try."

"First, we need to construct two more sets," Caleb said. "And we don't have enough Y-shaped branches so we'll have to hold them directly."

"We can do it," Dom said confidently.

The Karma Chameleons worked right up until the starting time to create two additional sets of branches for transporting the marbles.

"Hey, team," said Serena, who had been quietly constructing branch ramps up until that point. "I love how we are working together. I just want to make sure we all feel comfortable with this new strategy? It's a little risky, but I feel we can do it. Does everyone agree?"

A head nod or "yes" from each team member committed the Karma Chameleons to their plan. There was no time left to practice, however.

Ms. Allport called the group together and told everyone to get in place. Within seconds of the whistle blast, the Wingdings were yelling and arguing again. "Faster!" said one. "Slower!" bellowed another. It wasn't working.

The Dino Blasters went several feet and dropped all of their marbles to the floor, requiring them to start over.

The Galeontologists followed the "slow and steady" strategy that earned them 100 points, but they opted to move just one marble at a time, so they needed to make a lot of trips.

Iona considered the Galeontologists to be their main competitor and announced, "Hey look," then corrected herself, "Wait, don't look! Just listen. They are moving only one marble at a time then heading back to the starting line. If we use all four devices to move all the marbles in one trip, we'll win!"

Caleb added, "We should learn from what they did last time. They went quickly and lost their marbles. Let's go very slowly and carefully."

The team agreed. One step at a time, the Karma Chameleons advanced three marbles from the first section to the second and then the third, reloading each section with marbles as it became available. By the time they added the final four marbles, the team was in a groove. While the Galeontologists reached the finish line first, they had moved only one marble and there was still lots of time on the clock.

When the Karma Chameleons crossed the finish line with all ten marbles, the Galeontologists were the only other team to make it across the line even once. Iona led the group in a loud chant of "Karma, Karma, Karma, Karma, Karma Chameleons!"

When Ms. Allport blew her whistle to signify that the seven minutes had passed, the Galeontologists had carried four marbles across the line. The Dino Blasters had three, and the Wingdings had two. This brought the final score totals to 150 points for both the Galeontologists and the Karma

Chameleons. The Dino Blasters earned 100 points, and the Wingdings had 50.

Ms. Allport glanced out the window and said, "The sun has returned. Let's get some fresh air." She looked at her watch and announced, "You have 20 minutes of free time outside before we begin our daily science experiments. And by the way, there will be a chance to win points at the campfire this evening. The competition isn't over yet."

Dom felt relieved. The concept of a tie never made sense to him. Just before heading outside, Serena turned to the group and said, "We make a great team."

Everyone agreed.

CHAPTER SIX

After dinner, the teaching assistants set telescopes near the amphitheater. When the students arrived, they were excited to look at the stars and planets, but it wasn't dark enough yet.

The fire was roaring once again, thanks to Camp Discovery's groundskeeper. Mr. Marston informed the students that tonight's portion of the story was short. He wanted to give them plenty of time for stargazing.

Iona turned to Caleb and put on her best announcer voice. "Tonight's episode of The Bird Tale is sponsored by the planet Pluto. Pluto—the galaxy's cutest little ice ball."

"Actually, Pluto isn't considered a planet anymore."

Iona didn't have to say anything at all. Like all Parrots, she could say, "Seriously?" without even uttering the word.

"Oh, forget it!" said Caleb, letting his inner Parrot out. "It is an *adorable* little planet, Parrotfeather!"

Mr. Marston began, "Last night, we learned the second question of the Chameleon Code. Let's rejoin our travelers and see if they're ready for the third question."

The four emissaries emerged from their tents encircling the fire pit. Nightowl, of course, had staked her tent farther away from the fire than all the others. Owls all knew that a gust of wind in the wrong direction could spray hot embers onto their flammable tents and she wanted to be safe.

"Good morning, everyone. I trust you slept well," the Ambassador said.

"I did," Dovetail responded. "Thank you."

"Before we continue, some news. I received word that Vulturan raiding ships have been spotted sailing towards the Owl Kingdom, just west of the Dove homeland. In addition, our scientists announced their predictions for this year's summer storms: they will be even windier than last summer's. It seems to me that bringing Aviara together is more important than ever before."

Eagleye jumped into business. "Well let's get down to it. Last night, we talked about the first two questions of the Chameleon Code. What's next?"

The Ambassador said, "Join me," as she gestured towards four chairs surrounding the fire pit.

The emissaries settled in. "The first two questions are about you as an individual: *Which bird am I?'* and *'Is my bird at its best?'* The next two questions are about others."

The Ambassador retrieved a black iron tea kettle that she had placed on some smoldering embers. After pouring a cup of tea for each of the emissaries, she continued. "The third question is, *'Which birds are they?'*"

"What does that mean?" Eagleye responded. "Who are they?"

"Everyone," the Ambassador said.

"They are everyone?" Eagleye asked.

"Exactly," the Ambassador grinned.

"I think Eagleye is saying that he needs more information," Nightowl clarified.

The Ambassador couldn't hold back her laughter. "I figured. Think about it this way. The Chameleon Code isn't just about knowing yourself. It's about knowing others. And not just a few others. The Chameleon Code is about understanding everyone you meet, know, and love."

The Ambassador took a long sip of her tea and glanced at the rising sun.

"When you are home within your kingdoms, you know that everyone in the Dove Kingdom is a Dove. Everyone in the Owl Kingdom is an Owl.

The same goes for the Parrot and Eagle Kingdoms as well. But if you travel away from home and encounter someone in a distant land, how will you know which bird they are? You must become skilled at birdwatching. When you meet someone new, you must be able to quickly determine their bird type. If you can do that, you will instantly know how to talk with them. And so, the third question of the Chameleon Code is, *'Which birds are they?'*"

"But how are we supposed to know which birds they are if they are not in their kingdom?" Nightowl asked.

"Recall how the four of you interacted on your journey here. Nightowl, since you asked the question, let's start with you." The Ambassador turned to the other three emissaries. "Give me one positive word, and I mean positive, that describes Nightowl."

Parrotfeather spoke first, "Logical. Her logic impresses me."

"Detailed," Eagleye added. "She shares lots of information and seems very accurate."

"Thoughtful," Dovetail added. "I can feel that she likes to think things through."

Nodding her head, the Ambassador said, "And so, if you meet someone who is logical, detailed, and thoughtful…"

"And asks a lot of questions," added Eagleye.

"Yes, and asks lots of questions—that person has a lot of Owl energy within them, and thus we can say that they are an Owl."

The Ambassador turned to Eagleye. "Let's talk about the Eagle Kingdom. More specifically, Eagleye."

"Oh, she's all about results," Parrotfeather said. "She likes to get things done and takes charge to make it happen."

Eagleye nodded proudly.

"And very decisive," Nightowl added. "She makes quick decisions. I'm not good at that."

"And she's direct," Dovetail shared. "I respect that. She tells it like it is. That's hard for me."

With a smile, the Ambassador said, "Therefore, if you meet someone who focuses on results, is decisive, takes charge, and is direct, you can bet you are in the presence of an Eagle." The Ambassador looked up at the colorful sky, as if there was some invisible sign only she could see. "There may be hope for the four of you yet. Let's talk about the Parrots."

"That's perfect because they love talking," Nightowl said.

Parrotfeather laughed. "You got that right!"

"And they always look to the bright side. No matter what is happening, they stay positive and cheerful," Dovetail added.

"I like how the Parrots get people excited about getting things done. They have a lot of energy and are enthusiastic about everything they do," Eagleye added.

"Very good," said the Ambassador. "Now tell me about the world of the Dove. What is Dovetail like?"

Eagleye answered quickly, "Considerate. He makes sure that other people are happy and heard."

Parrotfeather added, "He's a great listener. I could use a little of that. I'm more of a talker."

"I hadn't noticed," laughed Eagleye.

Nightowl addressed Dovetail directly, "I gather that you're sensitive and sincerely care about how others feel."

"I do care about how people feel," Dovetail confirmed.

The Ambassador nodded with approval.

"Considerate, caring, good listener, and sensitive. Sounds like a Dove to me."

Dovetail humbly agreed.

The Ambassador paused to let everyone's words sink in, then continued, "In Chamelia, we have an expression: 'Everyone is a book if you know how to read them.' If you pay attention, and I mean truly pay attention, you can figure out which bird they are."

"So, you're saying that if we understand ourselves and others—and try to be our best selves, as you said yesterday—we will be able to solve the great problems that face Aviara?" Nightowl asked.

"Precisely," the Ambassador said.

"I'm up for anything that will allow us to achieve our goals," Eagleye stated.

"Practicing the Chameleon Code will help you do just that."

As if thinking out loud, Dovetail added, "We'll be able to help everyone who needs it."

The Ambassador nodded warmly.

"And we'll have fun again!" Parrotfeather cheered.

"With flying colors!" said the Ambassador. "Now let's have breakfast. I have prepared the

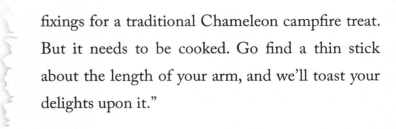

fixings for a traditional Chameleon campfire treat. But it needs to be cooked. Go find a thin stick about the length of your arm, and we'll toast your delights upon it."

Mr. Marston smiled. "Ya know, that sounds like a great idea. How about you do the same? But before you go find a stick so you can toast marshmallows, we need to determine the winner from today's dinosaur egg challenge. Remember the other night when you each selected which bird kingdom you would have chosen to live in? Well, let's see if you can remember the bird style of the people on your team. It's time for you to answer the Ambassador's third question, *'Which birds are they?'"*

The teaching assistants handed out pens and paper as Mr. Marston continued, "The sheet of paper you just received contains the names of your team members from today's challenge. On the blank line next to each person's name, write down which bird kingdom you think that person selected. In other words, *'Which birds are they?'* For each one you get right, your team gets 10 points that will be added to your total from earlier today."

Everyone wrote down their answers and handed in their sheets to be tallied by the teaching assistants. Mr. Marston continued, "On the table behind you, there is hot chocolate and jumbo marshmallows. Find yourself a stick and enjoy!"

Iona was impressed with Caleb's technique. Somehow, he seemed to get a perfect light brown color that surrounded the entire marshmallow. She realized it was his Owl nature that allowed him to create a perfect treat so patiently.

As for Caleb, he was more impressed with Iona's stick than her toasting technique. Evidently, Iona had kept several feathers she found earlier in the day and attached them to her stick. Her first marshmallow burst into flames and plopped into the fire.

Iona noticed that Caleb was admiring her handiwork and said, "Hey, if I'm going to light marshmallows on fire, I'm going to do it in style."

"Parrotfeather would be proud," Caleb joked.

"I think he would," Iona replied.

They both laughed and loaded their sticks with another marshmallow.

After the group had its fill of marshmallows, Ms. Allport doused the fire with water. "While stargazing, a fire is a lot like a bird style," she said. "If it shines too brightly, it blinds the stargazer and hides the wonders of the night sky."

For the next hour, the students gazed at the craters on the moon. Iona claimed to have spotted Pluto. Caleb wanted to share the many reasons why she definitely didn't see Pluto but restrained himself. Why spoil a Parrot's fun?

Just before they returned to their cabins, Mr. Marston announced that the Karma Chameleons were victorious. They were correct that Caleb had chosen the Owl Kingdom. Dom had selected the Eagle Kingdom. Serena had chosen the Doves, and Iona had picked the Parrots. They were right about the four other Karma Chameleons as well.

They successfully answered the Ambassador's question, *"Which birds are they?"* and won the day's challenge.

As the evening came to a close, Mr. Marston left the Galen 5th graders with a hint about tomorrow's activity. "I suggest you get a good night's sleep. Tomorrow, your Chameleon wisdom will be put to a test."

CHAPTER SEVEN

The students woke up to blue skies and Camp Discovery's resident birds cheerfully singing and fluttering about the tree branches. They dressed quickly and rushed to the mess hall for the day's big activity: the legendary Treasure Hunt, revered by every former Galen 5th grader.

Following a breakfast of waffles and bacon with amber syrup, the students gathered outside the mess hall. Iona and Serena were talking about how much they were enjoying the week. Well, Iona was talking. Serena was listening politely. Ms. Allport, standing nearby, was delighted to hear they were having a good time. Then again, Iona seemed to enjoy everything she did. Today's t-shirt said it best: "If life's not fun, you're not doing it right."

"That's a Parrot shirt if I ever saw one," thought Ms. Allport.

She gathered the group together and didn't need the whistle to get everyone's attention. They were eager to begin. She told them that somewhere hidden on the grounds of

Camp Discovery were clues leading to a treasure. If at any point they felt like they wanted to give up searching for it, they could head to the lake for their choice of water activities.

Dom turned to Caleb. "What does she mean by 'give up?'"

"With an Eagle on our team, we will never surrender," Caleb said, making good use of the Chameleon Code.

Ms. Allport continued. "You will work with the same teammates from Monday's orienteering challenge. Find them now."

When Serena, Dom, Iona, and Caleb were back together, Iona couldn't contain her glee. "The Karma Chameleons rise again!"

Caleb corrected her. "Technically, not all eight members of the Karma Chameleons are here." Then he realized he was shining his Owl light a bit too bright and added, "But go Karma Chameleons!"

After the teams assembled, the teacher added, "All of the clues are located within Camp Discovery, so stay within its boundaries. Here is your first clue: 'There is great wisdom within the Kingdom of Chamelia. Go there to receive guidance.' From here on out, you are on your own."

The students pondered the clue. Many looked confused since Chamelia is an imaginary place in Mr. Marston's Bird Tale. It didn't take long for the Wingdings to abandon their search and head to the lake.

Caleb, chin resting on his knuckles, soon lifted his eyes to meet his teammates. "Let's think about this. There were four bird kingdoms and a fifth kingdom for the Chameleons. Where would that kingdom be?"

Serena spoke softly, "What if we map the kingdoms to our camp?"

"What do you mean?" Caleb asked.

"If the camp is sitting on the continent of Aviara, Chamelia would be at the center," Serena explained.

"That's it!" Iona announced. "We need to find the center point of the camp. Caleb, do you still have the map that we used during orienteering?"

"I do. We were allowed to keep it and I figured it might come in handy."

"Ya know, having an Owl on the team is even better than GPS," said Dom. There was no time to waste for the Eagle. "Let's get it."

The team retrieved the map from Caleb's cabin. To no one's surprise, it was neatly tucked away with his belongings, just where he expected to find it. Caleb studied the landscape, "What if we take this map and fold it in half. Then we fold it in half again. The point at the center of the paper would be close to the center of Camp Discovery. That's where Chamelia is located."

The group agreed and Caleb identified their first stop.

"This would be a lot easier if we had a compass," said Caleb.

"Yeah, but we returned all of them," Serena noted.

Caleb stood deep in thought. Everyone was waiting patiently for him to share what he was thinking until Dom broke the silence. "What's up?"

Caleb remembered Ms. Allport explaining how to make a wilderness compass. "I'm not certain, as I've never done this before, but I think I can make one. Give me a minute."

Caleb wandered off to gather supplies. When he returned, he was holding a paperclip, a leaf, and a cup of water. "Remember, Ms. Allport said, 'In case of emergency, you can make a wilderness compass if you have the right materials.' Well, here are the materials. I think."

"How do we do it?" Iona asked. "I probably was talking while she was explaining that."

"You were running through a list of your favorite ice cream flavors," Dom confirmed.

"Great, now I want ice cream," Iona shrugged.

Serena shrugged back to convey that it was okay.

"If I am doing this right, we put the leaf on the water in the cup. He straightened the paper clip and then folded it back and forth until it broke in half, as the paper clip was longer than the diameter of the cup. "Next, we need to magnetize the paper clip. Any ideas on where we can find a magnet?"

Dom suggested, "The bathroom stalls close with a magnet. Can we use one of those?"

"Perfect!" Caleb exclaimed. "I'll get it."

He returned holding the magnet and a screwdriver.

"What's the screwdriver for and where did you get it?" Iona asked.

"I used it to remove the magnet, and I got it from my emergency kit," Caleb said matter-of-factly.

"You brought an emergency kit?" Dom asked.

"Didn't everyone?" Caleb replied.

"Thank goodness for Owls!" said Serena. "They think of everything."

They determined the north end of the magnet by placing it on the leaf in the water. The direction they traveled for orienteering was northwest, so the end of the magnet aiming close to that direction must be its north end. Caleb stroked the paper clip with the north end of the magnet exactly 40 times as instructed by Ms. Allport. To their delight, the paper clip began to spin slowly.

"This is sweet! Now we know where to go," Iona cheered.

"It'll be 1,200 steps away," added Caleb.

"How do you know *that*?" asked Dom.

"Weren't you listening to The Bird Tale on our first night? Nightowl counted her steps to estimate distance. Camp is a mile long and a mile wide, and if my stride is similar to

Nightowl's, that's 2.2 feet per stride. That means it's 1,200 steps from here at the edge of camp to the center."

"Dude…" said Iona. "I can't even."

Using their map and homemade compass, they set out for Chamelia.

Before long, Iona spotted their target. "Hey, there's Mr. Marston! I'll bet he's got our next clue!"

When the group arrived, their teacher was sitting on a beautifully carved log. It couldn't have been comfortable. "Welcome to Chamelia," he said. "How did you find me?"

The group explained how they made a wilderness compass and used the map to locate the Chameleon home at the center of camp. Mr. Marston beamed with pride. "In addition to your next clue, I will give you a hint that will help you on your journey." He got down on one knee and gestured for the kids to move in closer. He whispered, "Be the Chameleon."

"Be the Chameleon?" repeated Dom loudly.

"Be the Chameleon," whispered Mr. Marston again.

"Can you tell us anything else?" Caleb asked.

"I can. There is a shed near the water in the Dove Kingdom. Your next clue awaits you there."

"The lake is in the southeast," Caleb thought to himself. "There's a shed where they keep life preservers and canoe paddles. That must be it."

"You will find someone at the shed," Mr. Marston

continued. "He may not seem willing to help you, but remember what I have told you. Be the Chameleon."

"Thank you, Mr. Marston," Serena said before the group set out towards the Dove Kingdom.

Along the way, they passed the groundskeeper who was trimming some shrubs to perfection. "So cool!" Iona shouted out as she passed by.

As usual, he shrugged and kept working.

Having spent time in the canoes, the group knew where to go. They moved through the forest feeling confident they were on the right path. After reaching the lake, they spotted the shed nestled along the beachfront. And in front of the shed sat one of the teaching assistants. Members of both the Wingdings and Dino Blasters were nearby in the water. As usual, the Wingdings were yelling about something.

Dom took charge. He asked rapid-fire questions without even taking a breath. "So what is the next clue? Are we the first ones here? Where do we go next?"

Remembering to stay in character, the teaching assistant said, "How are all of you? I'm so glad you are here."

Dom immediately replied, "We're good. Do you have a clue for us?"

"What's the rush?" the teaching assistant replied.

Serena stepped between Dom and the teaching assistant and turned to the adult. "Can you excuse us for a moment?"

The teaching assistant gave a polite nod.

Out of earshot, Serena began, "I'm thinking about what Mr. Marston said to us before we left, 'Be the Chameleon.' I feel like that was a big clue. And if that's correct, what would a Chameleon do right now?"

"I know," Dom stated confidently. "Think about the Chameleon Code."

"What do you mean?" Caleb asked.

"Question one: *'Which bird am I?'* Well, I'm an Eagle."

"Okay."

"Question two: *'Is my bird at its best?'* If I'm being honest, I am probably being a bit too Eagle right now, but I'll work on that later."

"So far, so good," Iona chimed in.

"Question three: *'Which bird are they?'* In this case, the person we are talking about is the teaching assistant and I'm guessing he's a Dove."

"I would agree with that," said Serena. "He had a gentle smile and sincerely wanted to know how we were doing."

"But we don't know question four yet," Caleb replied, "and I bet that would help us right now."

"We don't know the fourth question, but I have a feeling it has something to do with how we treat others," said Dom. "I just treated a Dove like an Eagle and that didn't get us anywhere. Chameleons would adapt to the person they are talking to and I wasn't being very Chameleon-like. We need to adapt and treat the teaching assistant as if he were Dovetail."

"Huzzah! You're onto something," Iona said with her usual optimism.

"I love that," said Serena. "We were speaking to a Dove, so we should have spoken like a Dove."

"That's very logical," Caleb agreed. "We need to go back to the teaching assistant and be the Chameleon."

"I'm happy to do it," Serena said. "It would probably be easiest for me since I am from the Dove Kingdom, after all."

Dom put up his hand before anyone else could speak. "I'll do it. Since you are a Dove, you wouldn't be acting like a Chameleon. I'm an Eagle. By acting like a Dove, I will be adapting to the person I'm talking to. Remember, Mr. Marston said, 'Be the Chameleon.'"

"Can you do it?" Iona asked.

"Of course," Dom replied. "I can do anything."

Serena held her breath as Dom approached the teaching assistant. "It's so nice to see you," Dom began.

"It's nice to see you too."

"Have you been enjoying your week?"

"I have. What a great group of kids you all are."

"Is this your first time here at Camp Discovery?"

"It's my second time. Last year was my first."

The polite conversation continued, and Dom held it

together longer than Serena expected. After several minutes, Dom made his move. "If it's not too much trouble, you know we are on a treasure hunt. Would you happen to have any information that can help us?"

The teaching assistant nodded with approval and said, "In fact, I do have some information that could be of some assistance. Head into the deep forest where nature lovers go. Play with the animals that leap to and fro."

"Oh, oh, oh! I know, I know! The Nature Center," Iona blurted. "She's talking about the goats. Do you think the goats are still there? I love the goats!"

"Probably. Where else would they be?" Caleb asked. "But either way, I think you are correct. And I love your Parrot enthusiasm."

The team remembered where to pick up the trail to the Nature Center. They were on their way. Iona charged ahead of everyone and encouraged the team to hurry up. They walked through the densest part of the campground through thick stands of pine trees. They hurried by a koi pond where the fish remained motionless in the perfectly clear water. The trimmed rose bushes around the pond seemed like something the attentive groundskeeper would create. Serena paused for a moment to take in the tranquil beauty.

When they arrived at the Nature Center, a teaching assistant was sitting next to a tripod holding a camera. In her hands was a field guide of the region's birds and around her neck was a pair of binoculars.

In her excitement, Iona proclaimed to her teammates, "I got this!" She then turned to the teaching assistant and asked, "Whatcha doin'?"

"Bird watching," replied the teaching assistant who raised a finger to her mouth indicating they needed to talk quietly.

Iona, not used to adjusting her volume, asked loudly, "See anything interesting?"

A small blue bird with white markings took flight from a nearby branch.

"I have seen three species of sparrows, two robins, a blue jay, and a small yellow bird that I have not yet identified in the guidebook."

Caleb sensed that Iona was about to ask for help with their treasure hunt when he asked his teammate if they could chat. When he pulled Iona aside, he asked, "Which bird do you think she is?"

"I'd bet she's an Owl." Iona's eyes widened. "Uh oh."
Caleb nodded.

"I see where you're going. She's an Owl and I need to be the adaptable Chameleon and talk to her like an Owl. I was being a Parrot."

Caleb was about to give Iona some advice, but she was already off to win over the teaching assistant. Before she spoke, she took a deep breath and readied herself to be the Owl. "Can you tell me more about the yellow bird? I can look through the field guide to find it, if you would like."

The teaching assistant quietly described the bird and Iona began flipping through the pages. A rush of energy ran through her and she was about to exclaim, "Is this it?" when she dimmed her Parrot energy, slowed down, and quietly posed the question.

Iona asked detailed questions about the birds she observed—about their coloring, habits, songs, and nests. She then asked the teaching assistant to show her how she was tracking the birds she observed. Iona was impressed to see an organized book with check marks, dates, and locations.

The teaching assistant recognized just how much Iona had flexed her inner Owl. "Thank you for your interest in what I am doing. I believe I can help you on your quest. At the top center of the Eagle and Parrot Kingdoms, you will find your next clue. And it's a big one. Or at least a tall one. Good luck." With that, the teaching assistant lifted her binoculars to her eyes and scanned the forest.

The group regathered far enough away to avoid disturbing the birds. Iona deserved the space to be herself after that Chameleon performance.

"What do you think that means?" Serena asked.

"If we think of Camp Discovery as a map of Aviara," said

Caleb, "the Eagle Kingdom is located in the northwest and the Parrot Kingdom is to the northeast. I believe she just told us that the next clue is at the top center of the map."

"I might know where to go," Serena said. "When we walked in search of the flag while orienteering, we saw a tall, fire lookout tower in the distance. Since were in the northeast at the time, that tower is probably located at the top center of Camp Discovery. Do you think that could be it?"

"Sounds logical," Caleb confirmed.

"Let's go," Dom directed.

"Yessir, Eagleye," Iona saluted.

The group charged forward as Iona entertained them with a running dialogue of interesting things along the way. Her imitation of a British narrator from a nature TV show wasn't half bad.

During a pause in the show, Serena walked alongside Dom. "I'm curious about something. Can I ask you a question?"

"Of course," Dom replied.

"What was it like to speak like a Dove? I mean, since you are really an Eagle, was that hard?"

"I wouldn't say it was hard. It was more tiring than anything else. I had to think about what I was going to say, and that took energy. I guess it shows that we can be like the people from any of the bird kingdoms. It just takes a little effort,"

Dom concluded. "Why do you ask?"

"We're headed towards the Eagle and Parrot Kingdoms, and I'm feeling like it's my turn to be the Chameleon."

"You can do it," Dom said. "If you have to be the Eagle, just ask yourself, 'What would Dom do?' Then do that."

Serena felt comforted. "I will. Thank you."

Dom nodded. "Good talk."

"There it is!" Iona called back to the group as she pointed ahead.

Caleb turned to Serena. "I think we're up."

Just then, something dawned on Serena. "Do I have to climb the fire tower? I'm not too fond of heights."

"You can do it," Iona reassured her. "You can do anything!"

When they reached the base of the tower, they saw two teaching assistants. One was halfway up on a landing. The other was at the top on a platform.

Serena thought for a second about what Dom would say. She turned to Caleb. "Let's go."

"That's the spirit!" Iona cheered.

Caleb and Serena began their climb. After taking a few steps, the teaching assistant halfway up on the landing shouted to the pair, "Hey there, you two! Come on up. The view is amazing!"

As they got closer, the teaching assistant called out again, "Just a few more steps!"

When Serena and Caleb reached the teaching assistant, he high-fived the duo and welcomed them to the best view in the forest. Caleb recognized the Parrot energy and whispered to Serena, "I've got this one."

"What a sight!" said Caleb. "Do people still use this tower?"

"They sure do. During the dry season, people watch for smoke from up here."

"What are we looking at?" Caleb asked.

The teaching assistant identified a few landmarks.

"I'll bet this view never gets old," Caleb said.

"It really doesn't. I could stay up here for hours."

"You lucked out with this assignment!"

"I really did!"

Caleb dialed up his Parrot enthusiasm for what felt like forever. Finally, the teaching assistant said, "I believe there is someone at the top who has a message for you. But only one of you can make the trip."

Serena stood tall. "I'll go."

"Awesome!" the teaching assistant replied. "Have fun!"

"Fun, right," thought Serena. With her eyes, she followed the steps to the high, narrow platform. She pressed her foot to the first step.

"Be the Eagle," she whispered to herself. "I can do this. I am Eagleye." When she stepped onto the platform at the top, the teaching assistant was looking out in the distance. Without turning his head, he grunted, "Hey."

Serena turned up her Eagle energy. She planted her feet firmly and asked, "See anything that concerns you?"

"Nope," he replied. "All good."

"You look busy and you're doing important work. Can I take just one moment of your time?"

The teaching assistant nodded.

"As you know, we are on a treasure hunt and we are looking for clues. Is there any information you can provide us? If so, we'll be on our way and leave you to look for fires."

"I like how you roll," the teaching assistant replied. "As a matter of fact, there is. Return to where you began. The Ambassador sits on the treasure you seek."

"Thank you," Serena replied. And down she went. As she reversed her footsteps, she repeated the teaching assistant's words to herself. She didn't want to forget them and let her team down.

When she reached Caleb, who was in the middle of an animated conversation about the Hubble Space Telescope, she told him that it was time to go. They walked down the remaining steps side-by-side, each with a hand on the railing.

When they reached the ground, Serena recounted their adventure. "Here's what we learned. We need to go back to where we started. Evidently, the Ambassador is sitting on the treasure."

"Wait. What?" said Iona.

"Let's think about this," Caleb said. "We have two things we need to consider. Where did we start and who is the Ambassador?"

Dom replied, "The answer is simple. We went to the center of the map. In the story, that would be Chamelia. Mr. Marston was there. Therefore, he's the Ambassador."

"Aaaaaaand," Iona interrupted, "he was sitting on a pretty cool log. I'll bet that log is the treasure chest!"

"Caleb," said Dom. "Before we rush off to Mr. Marston, is there anything we're not thinking about? I want to tap into that Owl brain of yours."

Caleb thought for a moment. "Thanks for asking, but no. This plan makes sense to me. I think we should try it."

"Okay, then. Let's go."

The team half-walked and half-ran to Chamelia. When they arrived, Mr. Marston was waiting for them, but he was not alone. Ms. Allport and three teaching assistants were there with him. "Welcome back, my four emissaries," Mr. Marston said. "What brings you to Chamelia?"

Iona looked at her group with eyes that said, "I'm on it." She then turned back to the teachers and said, "I am Parrotfeather. And with me today are Eagleye, also known as Dom; Dovetail, who you might know as Serena; and Nightowl, who also goes by the name Caleb. We come to you today in search of treasure."

"Why do you believe we have this treasure of which you speak?" Mr. Marston replied.

Iona continued, "We have searched the four kingdoms, and the clues have led us back to you."

Ms. Allport said, "Remember what the Ambassador said when you first met him. If you are to receive the treasure, you must be worthy of these riches. You need to 'Be the Chameleon.' I suggest you talk with your team members. When you are ready, we shall entertain your request."

The group thanked the teachers and stepped away to speak in private.

"We have to get this right," Caleb said. "Being the Chameleon means adapting to the person we are talking to."

"But there are five people. How do we adapt to all five at the same time?" Dom asked.

Serena raised a single finger into the air. "Listen to this…."

After creating their plan, the group returned to the teachers. Dom began, summoning the best Dovetail he could muster. "We deeply appreciate all of the time you have put into this week. We have learned a lot about supporting each other and we made some great new friends, thanks to you."

Iona channeling Nightowl said, "I specifically want to

point out several things we have learned this week. First, we learned that we must understand our bird style. Second, we must try to be at our best—shine our light but not too bright. Third, we must understand the bird styles of others. And today, we learned that we need to be the Chameleon. Thank you for sharing your wisdom with us."

Caleb was up next. In his best Parrot voice, he exclaimed, "This was the greatest week...ever! And I mean, EVER! We had a blast! It was awesome! We will always remember the time we had here at Camp Discovery."

Serena closed out their request in her best Eagleye voice. She stood up strong, put her hands on her hips, and asked, "We come to you with one question: may we have the treasure?"

Mr. Marston looked left to the teaching assistants, who each nodded affirmatively. He eyed Ms. Allport to his right, and she nodded as well.

Mr. Marston addressed the team. "I believe you have earned the treasure." He rose from his seat and added, "You will receive your prize at tonight's campfire. For now, there are snacks waiting for you in the mess hall."

The four members of the Karma Chameleons high-fived each other and set off for the food. On the way, Dom stopped in his tracks. "Wait a minute. When we saw Mr. Marston the first time, his big hint was to 'Be the Chameleon.' Do you think he would have given us the treasure if we said what we just said the first time we saw him?"

Caleb laughed. "Some things are better left a mystery."

"And besides," Iona concluded. "The whole hunt was wicked fun. Now, let's grab those snacks."

CHAPTER EIGHT

Following their treasure hunts on the grounds of Camp Discovery (or their lazy day on the lake), the 5th grade class of Galen Elementary School prepared for the final installment of The Bird Tale.

Once everyone was seated in the amphitheater, Mr. Marston began. "In a moment, we will return to Aviara so you can find out what happens to our friends of the four kingdoms. If you recall, they faced four crises: one of security in which the Vulturans were threatening to invade Aviara; one of knowledge in which terrible storms threatened the continent and its homes, most of which couldn't withstand the winds; one of health in which a deadly disease endangered people throughout the land; and finally, one of spirit in which people were disheartened and fearful. It seems more important than ever that our bird friends find a way to work together. Let's continue where we left off, just after the emissaries discover the third question, 'Which birds are they?'"

The Ambassador began, "Before I reveal the fourth question, I'd like to ask, 'Why is it important to know which bird someone is?'"

Dovetail replied first. "If we know what bird they are, we can talk with them in a way they understand. In a sense, we can speak their language."

"Tell me more," the Ambassador requested.

"If I meet someone who asks specific questions or shares lots of information with me, I can guess that they are an Owl."

"And?"

"And then, like a Chameleon, I can adapt to what they need. I can speak the language of an Owl and provide the detailed information they prefer."

"Wonderful," the Ambassador exclaimed. "Simply wonderful."

"And if I meet someone who speaks softly and tries to be helpful, I can guess that this person is a Dove," Eagleye shared.

Anticipating the Ambassador's next question, she added, "And so I would speak kindly, listen carefully, and make sure they are comfortable."

"You are making my day," the Ambassador said proudly.

Not to be left out, Parrotfeather said, "If I meet someone who gets right to the point and seems assertive, I will assume that person is an Eagle. And I will be direct and speak confidently to them in return."

"Oh, I'd like that," Eagleye replied.

"I thought you would," Parrotfeather winked.

Nightowl added, "If I observe someone who has a lot of energy, is bursting with enthusiasm, and talks a lot, I can reason that they are a Parrot. And so, I can dial up my excitement and dial down the amount of details I share with them."

"Now you're talking!" said Parrotfeather.

"Well, look at that," the Ambassador said. "Look what just happened. You all just acted like Chameleons. You correctly explained how you would adapt to each type of bird. Instead of imposing your bird ways on others, you would treat them how they would like to be treated. And it's beautiful to see. Are you ready to apply what you have learned to your current situation?"

Eagleye locked eyes with the Ambassador. "Bring it."

The others agreed.

"Excellent. Imagine you are an Owl trying to

explain to a Parrot how to build a sturdy structure that can withstand powerful winds. How would you do it?"

Eagleye replied, "I would start off by getting them excited. I'd say something like, 'Who wants to build an amazing home that can withstand anything?!'"

"When can we start?" Parrotfeather replied with a grin.

"As an Owl talking to a Parrot, I would have to resist the temptation to provide too much detail. Parrots don't need to know the mechanics behind what's happening. Maybe we could make it a community event in which several families work together on each of their homes. It would be more fun that way."

"It's like you know me," Parrotfeather grinned.

"Very good," the Ambassador said. "And what if an Eagle wanted to explain to a Dove how to stand strong in the face of the Vulturans. How can the Eagle approach this?"

Nightowl requested, "Let me try," and turned to Dovetail.

"I would tell them, 'I know you want to keep your people safe from the Vulturans. You want to ensure that everyone is protected from harm and that your family is secure. Can we talk about how to project confidence when you stand up to the Vulturans? I have some thoughts if you're open to them.'"

"Marvelous!" said the Ambassador. "By communicating to the Dove in Dove language, you have become the adaptable Chameleon."

Mr. Marston left The Bird Tale to check in with the students. "Based on what we just heard and what you experienced today, can anyone guess the fourth question of the Chameleon Code?"

Caleb raised his hand. "We talked about this earlier in our group. We thought the fourth question must relate to being the Chameleon. Maybe the question is something like, *'Which bird is needed right now?'*"

Mr. Marston leaned forward. "You are close!"

Serena raised her hand and waited for Mr. Marston to call on her. "I feel it's something like, *'What would a Chameleon do?'*"

Mr. Marston's eyes opened wide. "That's it! *'What would a Chameleon do?'* Everyone, call it out," he instructed.

In unison, the 5th grade class of Galen Elementary shouted, *"What would a Chameleon do?"*

"Love it!" replied the teacher. "You are all awesome! Let's continue."

The Ambassador shared the fourth question, *"What would a Chameleon do?"* and explained, "Chameleons are like a mirror. They reflect the other person's bird style back to them. They adapt to the person they are talking to and speak that person's language. If you are speaking to an Eagle, reflect Eagle back to that person by talking like an Eagle. If you are talking to a Dove, reflect the Dove back to that person. Same for the Parrot and Owl. Treat people how they need to be treated instead of treating people how you want to be treated."

"That is powerful," said Eagleye.

"And logical," added Nightowl.

"And respectful," said Dovetail.

"And fun!" said Parrotfeather.

"I might just have to make all of you Honorary Chameleons," said the Ambassador with pride.

The group enjoyed one last meal together before returning home. They came to Chamelia as individuals hoping to help their own kingdoms. They left as friends who wanted to help all of the kingdoms.

Before they departed, the emissaries thanked the Ambassador for sharing the Chameleon Code. Just as they were about to leave, Nightowl had one last question. "When we met, you told us that you could not help us. I still do not understand why."

The Ambassador grinned. "To be exact, my Owl friend, I did not say I could not help you. I said that you did not require my help. When you were on your journey here, I saw you teach your fellow emissaries to build a stronger shelter. I watched Dovetail heal a sick traveler, and you all learned from his wisdom. I watched Eagleye stand strong against a threat, and she taught you how to do so as well. And finally, I watched Parrotfeather share his positive spirit with all of you, and you embraced his ways. You did not need me. You had already learned how to be Chameleons."

Nightowl nodded, and the group was on its way.

"How about we take a break for s'mores and hot chocolate?" Mr. Marston said. "You'll find chocolate bars, marshmallows, and graham crackers on that table. Help yourself. Afterwards, we'll find out what our emissaries learned and what happened to Aviara."

The group returned a little sticky but quite satisfied. They were looking forward to the conclusion of The Bird Tale. Mr. Marston began, "Let's see what happened to the four kingdoms."

After learning the four questions of the Chameleon Code, the emissaries returned home. They taught the four questions to their people and shared what they learned about the other three bird kingdoms.

From the Owls, they learned how to think logically through problems. Shortly after Nightowl returned from meeting with the Ambassador, her kingdom dispatched engineers who taught the Eagles, Parrots, and Doves how to reinforce their homes from the oncoming storms. When the wind and rain came, few structures were damaged. All the people of Aviara were safe from the storms.

The Doves taught the people of Aviara to listen patiently and respond with compassion. People learned how good it feels to help others. The Doves shared their knowledge of how to heal people from the new, mysterious illness. Although it swept across the land, most people recovered quickly, thanks to the Doves.

From the Eagles, the people of Aviara learned how to believe in themselves, speak with confidence, and stand in their power. The Vulturans arrived in massive ships, ready to storm Aviara's southern border. They believed the people of the continent were weak and would surrender quickly. They weren't prepared for what they encountered.

When they arrived, the Vulturans were met with a big surprise. Standing confidently on the shores of Aviara were tens of thousands of people. They stood defiantly with their hands on their hips, almost daring the Vulturans to come ashore. The Vulturans knew they could not succeed against such confidence and conviction. They retreated home, never to threaten any of the kingdoms of Aviara ever again.

The Parrots shared their eternal optimism, and people smiled again. They taught the Eagle, Dove, and Owl Kingdoms how to celebrate their victories. And celebrate they did. Aviarans learned how to maintain a positive spirit even when faced with the most difficult challenges. The Parrots taught everyone how to bring fun into daily life.

Now, years later, the four kingdoms are unified as one nation: Aviara. They work together to solve their problems, and they appreciate their differences. The Chameleon Code is now taught to children throughout the land so as they grow into adults they know how to talk to and get along with anyone they meet.

The Galen 5th graders broke into applause. Mr. Marston stood, then bowed with gratitude. He took a sip of hot chocolate and said, "We have one last order of business before we call it a night. Today, one of the teams found the hidden treasure. That means we have some prizes to award."

When the teacher rose from the log he was sitting on, Dom, Iona, Serena, and Caleb all realized that it was the same log he had sat upon when they met him at the center of Camp Discovery. He reached down and removed the lid from the hollowed-out log. He peeked inside and said, "Several members of the Karma Chameleons have prizes waiting for them. Should we give them their reward?"

Everyone cheered.

The four teammates walked to the front of the amphitheater and looked inside the log. There were dozens of rolled up shirts wrapped with either a red, yellow, green, or blue ribbon. Mr. Marston pointed to the prizes and said, "You may each select one."

Iona was about to reach into the log treasure when Serena

said, "Hold on."

Iona was so excited, she didn't hear her and grabbed hold of a shirt.

Serena gathered all the strength inside her and shouted, "Stop!" She recalled how Dovetail didn't speak up and share the instructions he received in his scroll. She thought about how confidently Eagleye would tell the other emissaries what to do. She knew this was an Eagle moment.

Iona jumped back in surprise, dropping the shirt back into the log treasure chest.

Serena looked at her teacher and said, "We need a minute before we collect our prizes." She then asked her team members to join her a few feet away. When they returned, Serena turned to the entire 5th grade class and said loudly, "Hey everyone, how many teams went looking for the treasure today?"

The group replied all together, "Eight!"

"And how many cabins do we have here at Camp Discovery?"

"Four!"

"And how many groups are here this week?"

"One!"

She placed her hand behind her ear, "I can't hear you!"

One!" they shouted even louder.

Caleb then turned to look at Mr. Marston. "Well, there

you have it. There is just one team."

Dom continued. "We were talking. And since there is just one team here," he looked at Serena to bring it home.

"We think everyone should get a shirt," Serena said assertively.

Mr. Marston, Ms. Allport, and all of the teaching assistants were beaming with pride. Mr. Marston replied without hesitation, "Well then, it seems like the 5th grade class has spoken. So be it! Come on down, everyone, and pick out a shirt. But before you do, the Ambassador has a word of advice. Remember the ribbons that were wrapped around the messages for the emissaries."

Iona nearly jumped into the air. "Listen up everyone, I think the shirts are related to the birds. I'm a Parrot, so I'm going to open one wrapped with a yellow ribbon. Here goes."

There was no stopping her now. Iona retrieved a shirt, slid the ribbon off, and she was right. She modeled her shirt for everyone to see. Laughter erupted when they saw a Parrot along with the words, "Let's talk!"

She turned the shirt around and printed in bold letters across the top, it read, "The Chameleon Code." Beneath that were the four questions: *Which bird am I? Is my bird at its best? Which birds are they?"* and *"What would a Chameleon do?"*

Dom selected a shirt tied with a red ribbon and was delighted to see a picture of an Eagle standing strong above the words, "Eagle Power."

Serena and Caleb opened theirs together. Serena removed a green ribbon while Caleb removed a blue one. Serena's shirt depicted a Dove that guided the reader to, "Be kind." Caleb's shirt had an Owl, and rather than ask the classic Owl question, "Whooooooo?" it questioned, "Why?" The shirts were perfect.

The rest of the group selected their shirts. Everyone was happy they won together, as one team, the 5th grade class of Galen Elementary School.

CHAPTER NINE

The next morning, Mr. Marston, Ms. Allport, and the teaching assistants sported t-shirts with the four birds and the question, *"Which bird are you?"* The students proudly wore their new bird shirts, though Iona had secretly hoped to wear her favorite "Ask me about my unicorn" shirt. She let it go, figuring there's always another day.

As the students loaded the bus for the trip back to Galen Elementary, Caleb spotted the groundskeeper kneeling in a flower bed with a pair of garden scissors in his hand. Caleb said to Dom, "He must be an Owl. Everything lines up so perfectly. It's incredibly impressive."

With a foot on the first step of the bus, Iona overheard Caleb's observation. She looked up and saw the fourth question of the Chameleon Code printed on the back of his shirt, *"What would a Chameleon do?"*

With eyes wide, Iona leapt from the bus and ran towards the groundskeeper with her long brown hair and Wild Orchid highlights flowing behind her. This time, instead of speaking like a Parrot, she slowed herself to a walk before reaching him and waited until he looked up. "Before I go," she said, "I wanted to tell you that I appreciate the time and effort you have put into making Camp Discovery a beautiful place. Every plant and flower is maintained with perfection. The shrubs look like they should be in a museum, as if they were sculpted by a master. Thank you for the care and precision you put into all that you have done here at the camp."

The groundskeeper slowly rose to his feet, looked her in the eyes, and said with deep appreciation, "It is I who should thank you. Many people have told me that my work is 'awesome' or that it 'looks great,' but I didn't believe they actually appreciated the time and effort that goes into making the grounds welcoming for all who come here. Your words touch me."

They shared a smile, and Iona returned to the bus. Once everyone was seated, Mr. Marston said to the students, "We are about to head back to where this week's adventure began. When you return, you may feel like a new person. The knowledge you have gained this week has made you wiser, more compassionate, and more respectful of others. I hope that during this week you learned about yourself and the people in your life. You discovered how to be the Chameleon and adapt to those around you. And remember, always strive to be your best."

The students broke into rousing applause.

Mr. Marston smiled and said, "I have one last question before we go, and I want you to think about it carefully before you answer. Which bird is the best?"

Serena answered, "How can one bird be better than any other? They're all good."

Mr. Marston beamed. "So, everyone, which bird is the best?"

Together, the 5th grade class at Galen Elementary called out, "All of them!"

Dom, Caleb, Serena, and Iona sat together during the journey home. As they talked about their week at Camp Discovery, Iona had visions of chocolate chip cookie dough ice cream waiting for them when they returned. For that matter, butter brickle would be great too. And cookies and cream is hard to beat.

ACKNOWLEDGEMENTS

There are always people to thank, as nothing great is ever accomplished alone.

To Traci, you have shown me the meaning of unconditional love and support. This book and everything I do would not be possible without you. To Gavin and Ben, you have taught me that no two children can be raised with one approach to parenting and that lesson fills these pages. Mom and Dad, thank you for inspiring me to write this book.

To my amazing team at Take Flight Learning, notably, Jeff Backal, Cathryn Plum, Andy Kraus, Dolores Woodington, Kerry Bayles, Rick Kauffman, Jim Di Miero, James Presley, and Brittany Mikulak, without you the birds wouldn't fly. And to all of those have been certified to deliver training programs based on the Eagles, Parrots, Doves, and Owls, I deeply appreciate that you are making a difference in the world by teaching people about themselves and everyone they know through the four birds.

To Richard Ellis and Edy McConnell, your gift of language makes this Parrot sound better than he should. To

Kaytalin McCarry, thank you for drawing the birds and this book into being.

A special thanks to those who offered a child's perspective before I shared this book with the world: Ariel Trezzi, Olivia Villalon, Zachary Plum, and Ava Plum.

A big mahalo to Dr. Tony Alessandra, Brandon Parker, and the team at Assessments 24x7 for everything you do to help children and adults answer the question: Which Bird Are You?

ABOUT THE AUTHOR

Merrick Rosenberg is the award-winning author of *Taking Flight!*, *The Chameleon*, and *Personality Wins*, three books about tapping into the power of your personality. Merrick founded Team Builders Plus, one of the first team building companies in the United States, in 1991. After the Eagles, Parrots, Doves, and Owls flew into his world, he created Take Flight Learning to help people understand themselves, be better leaders, and work together more effectively. He was worked with more than half of the Fortune 100 companies in the U.S. and around the world.

You might find Merrick strumming a guitar on his porch, playing with his pets, or doing the best he can in a yoga studio.

Learn more about the birds and determine your style at WhichBirdAreYou.com.

Discover the training programs based on the four birds at TakeFlightLearning.com or visit MerrickRosenberg.com to learn how people can be entertained and enlightened by Merrick's wit and wisdom at your next conference.

Made in USA - North Chelmsford, MA
1280552_9780996411066